ARROGANT RUCKING PLAYER

RUCKED BY YOU

SOFIA AVES

First Edition

Cover by the Cover Fling

PAPERBACK ISBN 978-1-923471-02-3

EBOOK ISBN 978-1-923471-01-6

Crazy love is the best sort.
It doesn't think. It doesn't wait.
Crazy love uses its whole heart to scream to a silent city
and doesn't care who hears,
as long as the one it adores listens.
And answers.

ATHOR'S NOTE

ARROGANT RUCKING PLAYER is set on my home turf, in Australia. Unlike most of my other books, I've let my Aussie language roam free amongst these pages. You might see a few words that you're not used to reading in my works. I'll do my best to explain them as I go but please be warned...they aren't typos, and neither is the spelling. The choice to use British (UK) English in this book came fairly easily. I've wanted to break out for a while now and this seemed to be the right book to do it with. Please enjoy this glimpse into my culture and a few of the experiences I've had. I'll see you at the end pages for another chat.

A forewarning: we order our meals differently in Australia. When we call it a main meal, we mean the biggest course there is, and at a steakhouse, we expect the plate to be well packed. Keep that one in mind for later.

Sofia xx

CHAPTER ONE

MASON

I never thought I'd grow sick of shit hot moms hitting on me, but it happened on the first day of summer Rugby camp. While most of my teammates were enjoying their off season in the Aussie heat, I volunteered to coach local kids during the first few weeks of their Christmas holiday break in December with sweat rolling down my back from the moment I got up in the morning. Not only did playing footy keep them off the street, but I got to stay in condition as well. Because damn, could those kids run rings around me.

Two of the mums waved as I jogged past. I gave a half-hearted finger wiggle back, juggling an arm full of cones and spare balls for today's first training circuit. A blur in red and black zipped past me at waist height, nearly knocking me on my ass.

"Whoa." I raised a knee in time to avoid crashing into the kid who could have taken out my entire pre-Christmas training contingent on his own. "With skill like that, you should be my new winger. Take my place on the team."

"Sorry." The kid paused long enough to give me a single word and sent me a crazy grin. His feet were on the move before I could take my next breath.

I raised an eyebrow. "Are you sure you're in the right place?"

"Brady's late. I'm sorry, too." A pretty woman—another mum, albeit a different sort from the perfect-in-pink ones who sat in the shade and posed like the cheerleaders they used to be a decade ago—dressed in black pants stained in several places trotted after the boy I assumed was her son. She swept wayward strands off her face. The rest of her long black hair was tied in a ponytail with a sheen that reflected the afternoon sun, the ends touching her pert butt.

"I don't usually allow lateness." I stopped juggling balls and tried not to perv on the woman mere moments after my vow to ward off hot mums. *Fucking fail.* I was as bad as the women I'd tried to avoid for the last fifteen minutes. "I know it's the first day of a new training clinic, and all, but—"

"It won't happen again." The woman spoke in a strained voice and with the harried grace of a mother used to apologising on behalf of a son who held her up getting out the door too often.

I recognised that tone, because my mother used it plenty of times on myself and my brothers back when I was a kid. Not that things like time mattered half as much as it did here compared to where I grew up, but still…

"I get it." I shoved a tower of cones under one arm and held out a hand. "Mason Hale. My mother used to sound a lot like you when she first came to Australia. I dragged her and my brothers here with dreams of playing football. Rugby," I added. That had been its own bone of contention. Soccer was my cousins' love.

The faintest smile curled the woman's lips. "Brady might appreciate that. I'll wait for him over there later, if that's okay," she added, already retreating into herself. "I have to go back to work. Sometimes I'll be able to stay, but I need to drop and run today."

"It's fine. We'll stay together, and pickup is in a few hours." I mentally kicked myself even as I offered her what I hoped was a non-threatening smile. *Judgy fucker that I am.* Of course the stains were from work. She probably spent hours in food prep or restaurants or worked somewhere similar. "The bleachers offer some shade in the afternoons when you can stay on days that you can. We're gonna be busy soon." I nodded to where some of the parents had set up house. "I'll send the kids over when we're done later. Has Brady got a water bottle?" He'd need it in the heat.

A grimace twisted her lips. "We forgot that too. I'll run over and get him something." She checked her wrist where she wore her watch on the inside. Not that the thin silver piece did fuck all to hide the pale scars or the purple bruising that discoloured her skin beneath.

My jaw set.

Not him, *we.* I watched her pretty face for a moment longer than was socially acceptable. Not that I was alone in my observations. "No need. There's a bubbler about. Brady can get water there. The kids use the fountain fairly often to wet down on a hot day."

"Alright." She pressed her hands together, watching her son run off. "He's a bit active, and he doesn't always listen—"

"Hey." I called her attention back to me. "You're good to go to work. I know we just met, but…I knew a kid just like him when I was young. He…turned out okay."

"Yeah?" Her eyes narrowed. "You?"

I shrugged. "Hyperactive-inattentive and still strong. I'll keep an eye on him. I promise."

Some of the tension left her in the next breath. "Thank you." She backed up a few steps.

It wasn't until she disappeared in the direction of the parking lot and I'd located my holiday training crew for the day that I realised that I'd never caught her name.

"Hi, Mason. Why don't you let me help you with that big bag of balls?" A single mum flashed too bright white teeth in my direction.

Three days into the training clinic, I knew less kid's names than I liked, but plenty of the mums sprang to mind on demand. All the ones I knew to stay well away from. I thought this one belonged to a kid I wasn't sure should be in the program that was supposed to cater for an underprivileged local socio demographic. I'd already caught myself being too judgy over Brady's mum and so I kept my trap locked shut on that topic.

"Uh, I'm good. Thanks." I turned to throw her a practiced smile I reserved for media that had been coached into me over the past three years, and came chest to erect nipples with a pair of protruding offerings plated up in super flimsy a bra that seemed determined to topple her breasts out of their encasing at any moment. "I'm really good." I backpedalled a few steps to increase my safety net. "Got it all in hand."

The mum took a step forward. "Are you sure?" Her grin widened.

I'm never volunteering for anything ever again. Not even for charity work.

No, that wasn't true. I'd really enjoyed the first few days of working with the kids these holidays so far. Just...not so much the parents, though I'd kept an eye out for my mystery woman. Not that I'd had much luck on that front. She'd been kept busy, dropping Brady off early each morning and running back to whatever shift work she did, all in black and no branding in sight.

Not that I was stalking her...just that I got my inner stalker on. In a safe way. Was there a safe way to perv on a mum who hadn't given me her name yet? I mean I could stalk her personal info, but that was crossing a line and... I groaned, dragging my hand over my face, and pried my eyes open.

A pair of erect nipples and too bright teeth blinded me.

"Urgh. Ah—" I stumbled over my tied tongue when the vision I didn't want assaulted me.

Not how the media team trained me to react.

"Fine." The mum flounced away, several things that shouldn't have flouncing along with her, while her hair and tits stayed fixed firmly in place.

I scrubbed my face with both hands and dropped my balls. "Fuck me."

"I think that was the point she tried to make." The soft tones of the mystery mum I'd been semi-stalking—fine, all out stalking—for the last few afternoons at pick up time without success drifted past me. "And you probably do actually need a hand now. Would you like these back?"

I peeled my fingers apart to see the woman I'd been crushing on holding my balls out in both hands.

"Yeah." *Gulp. What the fuck am I, a teenager in a school yard?* "Thanks for your help."

"You're welcome." She knelt to help me stuff

everything back in the netted bag. "Are they all that vicious?"

I laughed under my breath and managed not to look over my shoulder in case I got caught out by the rest of the super mum-cadre. "Ah, some," I said, cautious in my wording. "Not all, thankfully." Ballsing up, pun intended, I shot her a grateful glance and got my shit together. "I missed your name when Brady turned up on the first day." I strived for a casual tone.

She shot me a look. One that I bet Brady wilted under regularly. I joined him mentally.

"He's doing well," I strove for recovery.

Look the second was targeted my way.

I desisted.

Her lips quirked at one corner when I didn't sass her back, and her secret little smile was sweet and cute as hell.

"Nyla Jennings," she murmured, holding out a hand. "Watch that. I think I'm still covered in coffee dregs from a mishap earlier." She winced when our hands joined—mine a hell of a lot larger than her smaller, honey coloured one. Both came away sticky and a little gritty.

I shrugged. "I'm usually sweaty and muddy. There's nothing glamorous about my job." I eyed her curiously. "You work in a cafe— ah, a restaurant?"

She nodded and looked down at the stained apron still strung around her waist, the logo folded over, obscuring the business name. "It's not like I can hide it."

"Yeah. Right." I rubbed the back of my neck and came up smelling like coffee.

That's gonna be a fave from now on.

I didn't drink a whole lot of the stuff but I could go for a cuppa just to remember this conversation.

Damn, at this rate I'd be able to add *stalker* to my resume permanently.

"Mum!" Brady crash tackled Nyla at waist height the moment she stood, knocking the slight woman back a few steps. "Missed you."

"Easy there, bud. You don't want to hurt her."

I frowned, but she patted his head and kissed him.

"It's okay. I missed you too. Tell me you behaved well?" She looked between us anxiously.

"He did."

"Yep," we chorused in tandem.

"Hmmm." Nyla looked between us, that secret smile resurfacing. "I'm not sure I can trust either of you."

"I'm wounded." I pressed a hand to my chest.

"*Muummmm*." Brady grabbed her hand. "You promised burgers."

Her eyebrows raised. "I remember someone else promising that they would make their bed."

Brady ducked his head. "Yeah. 'Bout that…"

I laughed. "Maybe you can make it when you get him?" I tried to rescue him, knowing it wasn't my place at all.

Nyla shrugged. "We can do that. Thanks, Mason. He seems to really enjoy training with you."

"Loved having him here. See you tomorrow, bud?"

"See you, Mason!" Brady jumped twice for a high five I lifted, and left laughing.

I watched them leave, the field emptying out behind me as kids filtered off for the afternoon, heading away with their families. At the gate, Nyla stopped and looked back, giving me a small wave. That tiny gesture kept me going for the next three days until I figured I might catch her after work one time again.

And I wouldn't even have to get my stalker suit on for that one.

CHAPTER TWO

NYLA

"Another beer, love."

"Make it two." A hand cracked the table, and I was glad it wasn't my backside.

Ugh, I hated it when customers tacked endearments on the end of their wants and needs list.

"Order's up, Nyla!"

I waved a hand over my head and directed the next free waitstaff I had to the dinging bell that accompanied Sully, my best and most reliable chef who called out each order as it came up from the kitchen at the other end of the restaurant.

But his urgency wasn't the only priority I had to deal with right now.

"Table ten wants their birthday cake five minutes ago!"

"Fifteen has a complaint about the pepper sauce. *Again.*"

The four conversations aimed in my direction—five, if I counted Brady at the back of it all pointing to the upstairs toilet—clashed in magnificent fashion. I nodded to the latter and sighed at that last order, pushing away from the till where I'd been trying—unsuccessfully—to pre balance the cash because I suspected we were out. "I got the pepper sauce. Can you do the cake?"

So much for getting on top of things before they got away from me early in the night.

"I can do cake." Jenny ginned and waved on her way to the cool room.

"That's a load off. Thanks," I called out to her retreating back, although I doubted she heard me over the hubbub of *Cowboy's Pitstop*, a truly horrendous steakhouse themed restaurant situated on the southside of Brisbane.

I'd walk away from the restaurant, except that my sole source of income and Brady's inheritance was tied up in his father—and my more than frustrating ex's–silent share of the business.

Plastering on a smile I didn't feel any more, I

faced my next customer and took their payment by rote. "Lena, can you wipe down fourteen, please? Then there's a couple at the bar who have been waiting patiently," I murmured as I tossed a handful of silver into the tip jar. My fake smile stayed in place as I stared at the booking ledger for the mezzanine conference level on the floor above that had a full Saturday night striped through it for the next weekend marked out *Sanford Sentinels Christmas Party*.

I closed my eyes on a groan. Brilliant. All we needed was a club party on one of the busiest nights of the year, and we were already down staff with two out from sickness this week. I scrawled in *set menus* on the diary next to the booking, taking the choice away.

"You got it," Lena shouted in my ear over the hubbub in the bar. The rotund, bouncy waitress darted between tables, cloth in hand, menus already tucked under her arm.

My back ached already, and the night wasn't halfway done. A blur attacked me from the side. I held up a hand, but Lena hadn't doubled back.

"Mum!" Brady looped his arms around my waist. Chocolate smeared his mouth side to side in a goofy grin.

"Oh, my G—" I grabbed a handful of napkins and swiped his face, relieved the front counter was bereft of customers for the time being. "Brady. What has Chaz got you into now?"

Our chef had a French twang I wasn't sure he didn't put on for Brady's benefit and spoiled him rotten. A good thing too, as I often couldn't get a babysitter in time for extra shifts, especially on weeknights. Brady populated the kitchen when he shouldn't but Chaz and the kitchen staff didn't mind, feeding Brady's endless appetite and playing up to the kid with an infinite amount of energy.

And I was beyond grateful for their efforts.

"You're being good back there, right? You're not annoying the boys?"

"He is doing fine. We made you dinner, Nyla." Chaz, his voice stilted in an accent I was almost certain he hadn't been born with, presented me with two plates. One held chicken tenders and steamed vegetables drowned in mushroom sauce. The other contained a serving of chocolate brownie swimming in a pool of chocolate gooeyness.

I looked at both of them. "Is this what you've been doing?" I said sternly, fighting a smile. *Thank you,* I mouthed to Chaz over Brady's head as my son crash tackled me again at above waist height.

All the breath left me at once. Apparently those lessons were paying off.

"You are having a growth spurt, mister." I kissed the top of Brady's head. "Is it cake for me and veggies for you?"

"Ugh, *mummm*," he protested, wrangling the cake from me under no small amount of duress.

Hey, I wasn't giving up cake for no good reason, and certainly not without a fight when it came with chocolate sauce that looked that moreish.

Chaz smiled broadly and pulled a second serving of steaming chocolate brownie out of who knew where. I took the offering with gratitude, bowing to his finesse and placed it on the shelf behind me along with my dinner that I knew would be lukewarm at best before I got to it.

"Okay, why don't you boys head back to the kitchen and don't demolish all the cake before the customers get to it!" I called to their retreating backs.

The couple who had entered through the swinging saloon doors, one that hung not so artistically off its hinges and was just plain broken but thankfully didn't look that way, laughed.

"Sorry, I'm attempting to feed my child. Do you have a reservation?" I asked.

The rest of my night passed in a blur. I saw Brady

a few more times and managed to eat my vegetables and tenders though by the time I made it to my brownie it was a congealed, soggy, semi brick—the conundrums of chocolate kind—in chocolate soup.

I sighed and poked at it as I settled the til and came up short.

Well short.

Frowning, I set my barely touched brownie aside, if it was still worthy to be called such a thing, and recounted. *Nope, still short.* By a good two hundred flat.

That's too round a number to be a missed table.

And that happened. Hell, human error happened. As well as walking tables. But a round figure? That felt... Wrong. My gut knew that, and it wasn't the missing, congealed brownie at my side.

The broken saloon doors that looked nothing like anything had ever appeared in Australia's history, swung inward.

"We're closed," I muttered, my head still down as I recounted in no small amount of desperation for the third time.

Please be wrong. Please be wrong. Please, please, please.

But I wasn't. The money still counted out as short.

Which meant someone was skimming and I knew that, before I started. Had known for a while. What I didn't know was *who*.

Which meant one of my staff had stolen from me.

My singular bite of brown swooped in my belly.

"Fuck," I muttered.

"That's not very professional."

My head jerked up to meet eyes I never expected to see in the restaurant so late. Or in the restaurant much at all.

"Stuart." My voice flattened out at the sight of my ex. "What are you doing here?" I gripped the cash in my hand.

Fuck, fuck, fuck.

Of all nights for him to come in—I'd have to tell him we were short if he asked and then he'd—

What, blame me? Yes, absolutely. But more than that, he'd sack someone, because Stuart Jennings was an asshole. It's why I left him in the first place, and why Brady called him by his first name rather than Dad.

Kids had a way of working that sort of thing out on their own, funnily enough.

"I own the place, or did you forget?" He breezed past me as I closed the till and locked it, pocketing the key. Nothing else was going missing, though the only people left in the restaurant were myself, Brady, Chaz in the back singing opera at the top of his lungs and now Stuart who fixed himself a drink in the bar.

"That's all cleaned up," I protested. "Josie and Kesh finished up an hour ago. Don't screw with their system, Stu–"

"You don't tell me what to do, Nyla. No one does." Stuart poured himself a large glass of top shelf whiskey without marking the bottle or writing the freebie in the staff book, and headed toward the stairs. "I'll be up here until you leave. Then it's my night with Brady, or did you forget?"

Double fuckity. I had forgotten.

"I don't have a bag packed," I hedged. "It got crazy for a Thursday night, and we were short two staff."

"Your ineptitude is not my problem. Let me know when he's ready to leave."

I watched Stuart walk up the stairs with a drink that couldn't possibly allow him to drive, my protests dying in my throat.

I hate this life. What the hell do I have to do to leave it?

Tears welled in my eyes as I plunked myself on

my seat that till and unlocked the cash drawer, counting out the cash again.

And again.

Then I did the EFTPOS. At least that came up correct.

And then the tears began to fall.

A steaming, reheated, if slightly mangled brownie pushed in front of me.

"Chaz said to give you this before I go," Brady said in a small voice. "You forgot, huh?"

I nodded and held out an arm, not trusting myself to speak as I hugged him. "Gonna miss you, bud," I kissed the top of his head, realizing I used Mason's terms that I'd been listening to for the past week. "I'll pick you up after coaching, okay?"

"Okay, Mum. Love you." Brady kissed me all chocolatey.

I made a quick calculation in my head. "Do you think you could handle a phone soon? You're getting pretty responsible."

And then you can call me directly if you need me to come and get you. Panic closed around my heart at the thought of not having him for another day, or anywhere near Stuart.

"Sure, Mum. That would be great." Brady perked up. "One of the guys at school has this game. It's made of maths. You can send a guy sailing off cliffs when you dissolve things. It's really fun." He peeked up at me.

"Sounds awesome," I managed, sending Stuart a message.

NYLA: Brady's ready to go.

I waited for a response but I didn't get one. Just footsteps on the stairs a few minutes later. Stuart didn't even acknowledge me as he ruffled Brady's hair. My son stiffened slightly but slipped out of my grip all the same.

"Love you, Mum. See you tomorrow afternoon!" he called.

"Love you," I whispered to the swinging broken doors that encapsulated my life at that moment. The only thing that could fill the gap right now would be if one of them fell off.

I cooped up a mouthful of brownie as Chaz joined me at the counter, wrapping me in a big, end of night, chef-smelly bear hug. I didn't even care. It was human contact. And right now, I needed that more than anything else before I went back to my empty townhouse.

Alone.

CHAPTER THREE

MASON

"We're late. I'm—"

"Sorry. It's okay, Nyla. You don't have to keep apologising for life getting in the road of anything. We're not going anywhere." I high fived Brady and smiled at his mum.

"You remembered." She twisted her apron at her waist. "We were short staffed, and I don't make a habit of being late." The twisting increased.

I kept the frown off my face, fixating on hers by some miracle, but only just.

Who the hell ever hurt her to make her react that way overturning up ten minutes late to football practice just flew to the top of my shit list.

"Hey." I rubbed my knuckles across her upper

arm, the brief contact freezing her in place. But her twisting stopped and her hands relaxed, if only for a second. "Why don't you head up into the stands for a bit? It's shadier there and the afternoon will get pretty hot if you're staying."

Nyla watched me for a moment. Her mouth opened like she might say something else, then the moment passed. My hand dropped. She nodded, backing up, and headed to the seating area I had gestured to before. Without a good reason to keep her engaged, I turned to the kids I was supposed to be focused on for this session.

"Alright." I jogged the last few paces, noting the gaggle of kids knotted together, and where Brady stood off to one side. "Hey, you wanna help me put these out?" I tossed a stack of cones his way.

He caught them, looking surprised and grateful in one. "Uh, sure, Mace."

Feeling like a Jedi with a purple lightsabre, I pointed out where I needed everything to go and directed the other kids into a few line drills and warm up stretches. Brady joined in as soon as he was done setting out the cones for me.

"Let's start out with a circuit..."

I launched into the training program I'd spent the better part of a month working on to make sure it was both age and skill appropriate for the kids who had signed up, watching them work through the quick thirty to forty second rotations that tested their hand-eye coordination, ball skills, reflexes and endurance. After their first few sessions, their skills had levelled up and I adjusted each kid into groups accordingly. I wasn't surprised when Brady was my star player of the morning, but he was.

"You're doing great, mate." I passed him the ball. "Keep your passes tight, watch where the player is running, where he's going to be, alright? You've got this."

"Even if they're a lot bigger than me?" His brow furrowed.

I grinned. "Yeah, but you're faster."

He let out a whoop and darted around the much bigger kid pelting at him to snatch the ball out of the air and kept on running, well past the try line.

I cupped my hands around my mouth to holler down the field. "Don't forget to put it down or you don't score!" That hadn't been the point of the drill, but it didn't matter. They were having fun and Brady was suddenly the most popular kid on the pitch.

The kids were panting and sweating halfway into the session, but we'd all learned a lot about each other. Me, where everyone was at just by watching them, and them that I wouldn't be the kind of coach, even for the short term, who they could just push over and spend the next few weeks twiddling their thumbs in the grass or slouching off.

I loved this game, and if I couldn't get some of them to love it along with me by the end of the clinic, then I wasn't doing this part right.

"Alright, grab some water. You've earned the break."

I called a timeout on their tenth time around the circuit before we hit some more serious skills. Not that the upskill would be all that serious. I wanted the kids to have fun and enjoy the game, but I also wanted them to go home and be able to at least pass the ball better with their cousins and friends or whoever the hell they played backyard footy with over the Christmas school holidays.

Even with the late afternoon shadows creeping across the short mown grounds that browned off nicely until it rained again, heat beat down on the back of my neck. I flicked my collar up, glad I'd sent Nyla to the shady area. A quick glance her way confirmed she watched her son practice, though a small frown decorated her face.

I jogged backwards as I studied her, calling the kids back to their drills. A lump formed in my chest as I remembered the assumptions I'd made the first time I met her. Fuck it, I knew better than to judge anyone. Hell, people had done the same thing to me and my family when I first turned up in Australia, barely able to read and so behind in my classes that it took me two years in high school to catch up. I sure as hell couldn't sit still in a school room and I'd bet my month's wages Brady suffered the same issues as I had, sans the language barrier.

"Are you watching my mum?" Brady ran beside me like a little wraith.

More than that, he freaking well *kept up with me.*

I started and bit back a swear word a kid his age shouldn't hear but probably already had in some schoolyard or other.

"Ahhh—" *Busted.* I didn't need to add lying to my tally for the day already. "Yeah, I was watching your mum, kid. Just checking she's alright in the heat."

Not *checking her out,* but it came close enough. I'd just add *perving on married women to my list.* I winced. *Coach will have my ass if he catches me.*

"I check on her too. She works hard. Stu– My dad doesn't do much but piss her off."

"Language," I said absently. "Your Dad isn't around, huh?" I cursed myself half a second later for asking.

"Nah. He'll pick me up later in the week. Gotta look after mum. Hey!" Brady ran off to police one of the kids who had broken the rules of the game I'd set up a few minutes before our time out. The other kids scattered as he approached.

My attention diverted, I watched him work through the next set of drills, seeing a younger version of myself. Eventually, I pulled him aside as the games ended and sent the kids darting to the goal posts at the end of the field for a cool down run.

"Hey, Brady. You're doing awesome out there today." Giant brown eyes similar to his mother's stared up at me. How did I know that exactly? I told myself not to ask myself stupid questions so I wouldn't seek the wrong sort of answers. "But man, I need you to do something for me."

"Anything, Mason." The kid jigged on both feet, displaying a decent sense of balance.

I grinned. "I need you to practice the skills we did today."

His face fell a bit. "I dunno if Mum will let me throw a ball about in the townhouse."

A laugh ripped from my chest. "Yeah, I can understand that." I fished in my pocket for some spare change. "How about you practice this for me? I want you to put a coin on your elbow, and catch it again. Can you do that?' I demonstrated, placing the silver coin on my elbow, jerked my arm away, and caught it, then stacked another on top and did the drill all over again.

Brady's eyes widened. "Hell yeah! I mean, yeah." His voice dropped a few octaves when my eyes narrowed at his language. "I can do that, Mason."

"Good man." I ruffled his hair and dropped the coins into his palm. "I want you to do one other thing for me." *Several, actually, and the first is* 'look out for your mum'. But I only met her a few days ago, and it wasn't fair to put that on a kid who hadn't hit his tenth birthday yet. But if his family situation was what I suspected, it was going to happen anyway.

"Sure." Brady jiggled, clutching his coins.

I knelt to his level. At my height I still towered over him a bit, but at least we were closer to eye level this way. "Buddy, tomorrow I'll need your help when we set up. Putting the circuit out, helping out packing up."

"Maybe helping keep everyone in line?" He perked up.

I laughed out loud. "That might be my job. Don't take it away from me, okay?"

He laughed too and scampered around me, clutching his handful of coins. "Mum!"

I pivoted on my heel to find Nyla standing behind me, her arms wrapped around herself. "I hope you haven't been bothering your poor coach. He looks like he's had his hands full as it is."

"He's been great, haven't you buddy?" I grinned at Brady.

"I've been good. Promise." He grinned and chowed down on the handful of snacks his mother handed him from apparently nowhere.

"Uh huh." Nyla's lips twitched as she suppressed a fond smile. Those pretty brown eyes slid my way. "I saw what you did there, when he was..." She bit her lip, glancing down at Brady, but the kid wasn't listening, booting one of my spare footballs about.

"When he decided he'd take on the coach's roll for me?" I said easily.

She nibbled her lip and slid her hands into her apron pockets. "That. Yes. He...does it at school, too."

"Have the teachers talked to him about it?" I canted my head to one side, watching her reaction and had a good guess at what her answer would be.

She shrugged. "They don't seem to care."

"Mmhm." I watched Brady kick the ball about for a while longer.

"What is that noise?"

I blinked at Nyla, nonplussed. "What noise?"

"That throat thing you just did."

"Mhmm?"

"That one." She pointed a cracked fingernail at me, noticed, and hid it away.

It took everything in me not to grab her hand, pull her into me, and tell her not to hide just because she had a broken nail from work, because I could figure that much out for myself. But I managed to keep my hands to myself while her son circled us, kicking the ball about with a decent amount of skill.

"That sound." She nodded decisively as I rubbed my hand over my mouth, staring down at her.

A smile of my own threatened my lips. "That sound says Brady reminds me of me as a kid, and that his teachers should be doing more to help him out. But maybe I can. Not that I'm qualified, exactly." *What the hell am I doing?* This definitely came under *overstepping my bounds*.

"You...were, you *are* like Brady?" Nyla corrected herself as she stepped into my space hesitantly, pivoting on her heel to watch him play. "He's so—"

"Enthusiastic. Full of fun. And he means so well. That's the main thing, Nyla. Don't let that drive to be joyful turn inward, to anger. If it does—" I pressed my knuckles to my chest, over my heart. "It'll hurt like hell here."

"You're talking from experience." That was not a question. Her head canted to one side, the sunlight striking her cheek in a brilliant glow of golden skin. "Aren't you?"

That one was a question, and I had to answer her.

I swallowed. "Yeah. Let's say my teenage years sucked a bit, but I was lucky and had some good family who cuffed the back of my head when I needed it and pulled me into line." I forced a smile when she frowned. "You don't like the idea of that."

"It sounds violent."

"It was love." I grinned at the memory. "My cousins knew I was being a little shit, excuse my language." I winced after pulling Brady up for his all day. "And that I needed a reminder to behave like a human, just like everyone else. There's no room for pedestals in family. We're all the same. The day my call came that sent me to Australia, we all left together. That's what family is for." I shrugged as she watched me, her eyes dark and huge and luminous.

And glittering.

Nyla breathed out. "I wouldn't know."

My heart lurched in my chest. "Brady told me a bit about his dad—"

That's all I got out before she pivoted again, moving faster than I would have given her credit for, but apparently that speed was a trait Brady drew from his mother's side.

"Brady, it's time to go." Even her voice was abrupt as she covered ground in short, quick steps that put distance between us a hell of a lot faster than my brain could process.

I rolled my lips inward but didn't chase after her, flexing my fingers at my sides. Brady kicked the ball back to me. I caught it one handed returning his wave, though my mind flickered to the logo embroidered on her work apron that wasn't covered for once. *Cowboy's Pitstop,* along with the Busty Betty pictured next to the words.

Who knew, maybe I'd get lucky with the team Christmas party over the coming weekend. Because I had the feeling we'd be in the same space for a few hours, and I wouldn't have the distraction of twenty kids under my responsibility to take my attention off the pretty mum with the soul deep eyes that I wanted to drift away into.

Actually, I kinda didn't care if I fell into her with no safety net in sight.

CHAPTER FOUR

MASON

"Pass it. Faster! That's it," My coach encouraged the kids as I took the other side of the drills and lined them up.

The skills clinic grew hectic, both of us working the two groups we'd split them into earlier in the day simultaneously. Balls flew everywhere. There were more misses than catches, but the air fast filled with raucous shouts and laughter and...

That's what the game should be about at the kids' level. Encouraging fun and making sure they *wanted* to turn up next session rather than their parents bugging them out the door during their school holidays.

I lapped the group, making sure I earned an

extra layer of sweat to prove my worth to them as well as myself, and collapsed on the grass on my back as the last ball flew back into Leon's hands.

"Please thank Leon Nash for coaching us today!" I shouted at the top of my lungs. It wasn't much. My voice rasped at the end and I could do with a deluge of water for myself. The Aussie sun slammed me with late afternoon summer heat. Hell, I'll be shagged before the Christmas party later tonight, and I'd need a decent nana nap before I made an appearance at the restaurant. "I'm getting old," I muttered.

"Did you just call me old?" Coach stared down at me.

"I said *I'm* getting old," I called back.

"Not what I heard. What did you all hear?" He cupped his hand around his ear.

Showpony.

"You're. OLD!" the kids shouted back in perfect unison.

"Ahhh—" *This is so not good.*

"Well, go on then." Coach showed me his back.

Nearly twenty kids turn on me, over a week of school holiday drills beneath the blistering summer sun reflected in their eyes.

Double ahhh.

I squeezed my eyes and mouth shut as they began a game of *stacks on*, each kid piling one on top of the other with war cries over my torso until Coach called it and I was squished as deep into the dirt as I could possibly be. Actually, it might be mud now, consisting of my sweat and no small amount of my fledgling coach's pride.

Just awesome.

I checked the stands as I peeled my flesh from the grit but I didn't spot Nyla anywhere nearby. Brady loitered around, helping me pack up.

I nudged Leon. "Thanks for taking time out to help me today, Coach. It's good for the kids to meet a local legend." He didn't have to spend his time on us but he'd offered, and it did the kids good to see someone else's face apart from mine.

"National legend, thanks," he corrected me with a grin, and a slap on the back that stung. "See you tonight?"

I rolled my shoulders. "Yeah, I'll be there. Eight, right?" It had better not be any later, or I'd be in bed.

The team party culture hadn't interested me this season, a fact I knew Coach would be relieved to hear.

"Don't be late." He jogged away like the heat didn't bother him at all, and ignored the mums simpering at his silver fox style, along with his pay check and share in the club.

As far as I knew, Leon had been single for a long time and enjoyed the bachelor life with an intention to remain single, and no one else to share it—ever. His choices were his own. I stayed out of it. Whatever trauma the man carried had nothing to do with me.

That was a little different from how my life diverged from the rest of the party team of the league when I headed home each night to a small, outer suburbs house that filled with family at least one day of each weekend. Even so, it was far too big and quiet for me during the rest of the week. Hence the afterparty life to fill the space. Plus, there was sort of an expectation within the younger contingent of the team for it.

But I'd quickly found in my first year with the team that the hollow hours post midnight in clubs and spent with randoms in my bed didn't suit what I wanted, and... That I also had no clear idea of what I wanted in my life apart from a win each game during the season.

More like what I was supposed to need, but hadn't found yet.

Specifically, that what I hoped to hell was the

attention of the single mum I'd been dreaming about for the last week who wasn't there to pick up her son.

Because someone else stood in her place.

Brady waited beside a man in his late twenties, maybe early thirties, who I didn't recognise near the field gate. The man reached out, and he took a step back. My feet were moving before I made a plan to do anything, and my brain caught up with the program.

"Hey, Brady. Who's picking you up this afternoon? I haven't seen your mum about." I gave the guy an easy smile that he didn't return.

"This is Stu– He's my dad." Brady spoke to the ground and kicked up orange dust bunnies with the toe of his stained running shoe.

"Hi. I'm Mason." The fact that Brady hadn't given out my name didn't slip by me.

I stowed the information safely aside along with the way the rambunctious kid I'd grown more than fond of in the last few weeks curled into himself in a matter of seconds, putting distance between himself and the man who sired him, and stopped.

Literally, he stopped moving.

In nearly two weeks of hosting the summer football clinic, that was something I'd never seen Brady do. Unless it was for his personal form of preferred activity, or sleeping, I doubted it happened often.

"You're the coach, are you?" The man turned to face me, holding out a floppy hand that resembled some variety of fish pulled out of its environment. "Stuart Jennings. I'm Brady's father."

"Nice to meet you." I made contact with him for as little time as possible. The cool, moisture coated palm glided against my gritty once. I suppressed a shudder.

Pale eyes swept over me, taking in the dirt that covered my body, the ink decorating my skin. Hell, even down to what I wore and beyond. I met his gaze head on. In my lifetime I'd endured far worse from kids teasing me about where I was born, not being able to read and write like them when I first came to Australia, why my family looked different.

But in front of Brady I refused to back down before the bully I recognised this man to be.

Thank you for showing me who hurt Nyla. Stuart's wasn't a face I'd forget anytime soon.

But right now couldn't be the time to focus on the woman who had held my attention over the past weeks while I wished she stood before me instead of her ex-husband or whoever in the hell this man was to her.

"Are you okay this afternoon?" I asked Brady casually, like I did at the end of most sessions. Only this time I word my sentences a little more carefully.

The hell are you doing, getting involved in someone's family? But I knew what I was doing, and why. Because this kid was my responsibility until he left this field. If he didn't feel safe, he wasn't leaving with someone he didn't trust at all.

No matter who that might be.

"I had fun today, Mace," Brady said in that still muted voice that sounded nothing like the kid I coached.

I gritted my teeth. "Yeah? You did well. Are you good to practise those drills or do you need to grab any kit from my Coach before he leaves?"

I raised a hand and waved over my head, knowing Leon would be watching the exchange, too. Both of us had a radar for this sort of bullshit and any predatory behaviours. He could wipe the floor with my ass later for getting involved when I should back the hell up, but I couldn't force my feet to move away.

Stuart cleared his throat pointedly.

"Nah, I'm good. It's Stuart's day to take me home." Brady puffed out a breath. His fringe fell over his eyes, obscuring his face.

"Dad," Stuart corrected his son.

Brady didn't say anything.

I nodded when he didn't step away, either, or produce any sort of protest, at a bit of a loss on where to go with this. *Stay the hell out of family shit that's not your problem.* The voice in the back of my head snarked away at me, unfettered. But my stomach hit ground zero in a full body gravity slam that left me nauseated at leaving Brady alone.

"Alright," I said softly. Brady peered at me through his hair, and I swore my heart broke on the gravel beneath my feet. "I'll see you tomorrow, okay? We've got some new drills to work on and the Granny Grapple." I didn't have anything new planned, and I'd be hungover as fuck but I'd make something up just to keep my word.

"See you." Brady tramped away from me through the car park, heading for the only sports car left in the entire lot.

I smiled and waved when he turned back with a half-hearted grin and didn't feel any of it. Nor did Coach's huff behind me sting, knowing it would cost me an extra leg day or other punishment session of my own because he watched the whole event unfold. I'd have to fess my ass up because lying to the man was the worst idea I'd had all day.

But his words jarred me back into reality.

"You have a heart, Mace," he muttered.

"Yeah?" I raised my eyebrows, watching the sports car bunny hop its way out of the parking lot. *He can't drive for shit, either.*

Some part of me loved knowing that Stuart had extra flaws. The other half of me instantly worried for Brady's safety.

"Yeah." Leon coughed into his fist. "Just make sure you find the line of where to stop, and know where your involvement needs to end. Don't go too far and you'll be fine." His voice cracked at the end of his mini speech, and he coughed into his fist a second time.

I pivoted on my heel to face him. "Is that why you never let anyone in, never get close? Because you got involved one time?"

He sent me a crooked smile. "You just earned yourself two sets of Tour de Stade, my friend. Starting tomorrow morning before your clinic. See you bright and motherfucking early."

I clenched my teeth and smiled through the pain I could already feel radiating through my thighs at the concept of running the stadium stairs twice in any short period, even when I knew he'd rest me, though the kids wouldn't. "Sparrowfart it is."

So much for getting in that nap.

CHAPTER FIVE

NYLA

My antlers insisted on slipping over my face for the past hour. Wearing my hair out tonight had been a mistake.

Sweat rolled down my back under the blanket my hair formed in a packed restaurant that offered no reprieve or breath of air whatsoever with a broken air conditioner in sweltering December. The antlers and hair weren't tonight's only error. So was the polyester reindeer costume.

The tights itched with every step and the dress sat way too short for the football team who whistled each time I went up the stairs to the mezzanine level to serve them along with my troupe of reindeer servers who followed me around like we were ready to haul the sleigh for the night.

Only, I hadn't spotted Mason flirting along with the rest of his team mates no matter how hard I searched for him. Twice I checked the booking to make sure I had the right team, but from the matching ink several of the oversized boys were more than happy to show off to my girls—who I had to drag away to wait their tables—I was pretty sure I had the right club.

Just... No Mason.

"Lena, have the first courses been cleared?" I grabbed my best waitstaff as she darted past me.

Her cheeks blazed as she shoved what looked like a handful of something into her apron. "Uh huh. First course is away. Chaz knows. Mains are up soon for the set menu, then dessert."

"Okay." I turned on my heel and headed back downstairs, checking the other tables. Amazingly, the rest of the night ran fairly smoothly so far. I'd pulled one of my regular bar staff, Josie, out from her normal area and put her on the front desk while I helped wrangle the team upstairs for the event.

"How are you going?" I reached over Josie's head to dive into the emergency chocolate stash I kept behind the till for moments just like this one as my empty stomach rumbled on cue.

"I'm fine," she muttered absently, crossing out a line on the ledger where we kept our bookings, never having made the transition to a digital system. With so many hands in the pot, a paper based process seemed simplest. "We have two more parties left to come in for the night and we are *done*."

"That will be a relief. Any dramas down here?"

"Only your two boys in the bar having it out low key." She pointed the end of her fluffy pen bearing crossed, googly eyes over her head without looking up.

I glanced at the bar where Kesh handled two customers at once, passing over a pair of beers and taking change from another for a cocktail that she speared with a piece of spiralled lime.

Two tall figures hunched at one end of the bar. I didn't recognize the older man but there was no disguising Mason's dark, shaved head or the ink that peeked from the rolled sleeves of his white linen shirt. His collar was open at the top button as he half turned in my direction, gesturing to the open level upstairs. He looked so different in jeans than his usual sports coaching clothes minus a seasoning of mud that I had glossed over him more than once in my search for him this evening I suspected.

But I couldn't miss him now.

"I think they're starting to make people uncomfortable," Josie continued. "Wanna break it up?"

I stared at the gap between Mason and his friend where they sat at the bar. The rest of the patrons squished together away from them in the smaller space where we placed everyone waiting for tables once we ran out of rooms and reservations bulked up, especially on a Saturday night close to Christmas.

On a night like tonight.

"Right." It was time to pull my reindeer hooves up and behave like a big doe. "I'll handle it."

"I never doubted you." Josie turned away to greet her next booking that she swiped off the ledger with her fluffy pen. One of the googly eyes drooped and fell off the feather as I stalked across the floor, fixing my antlers firmly in place.

"Gentlemen, I believe your table is upstairs, if your drinks are ready?" I nodded to Kesh to make sure their order was complete.

All done, she mouthed back, grabbing two martini glasses. She coated them in sugar syrup, then dumped them upside down in a tray of salt crystals, already chatting to her next customers lining the bar.

Mason twisted about, the tight expression shifting into something more relaxed and like the version of him I recognised. "Nyla. I wanted to look for you after I finished here. This is Leon. He's my coach."

"Hi, Leon." I waved. "I'd shake hands, but I'm not terribly clean right now." I winced at how that came out and hoped for no snappy comeback tour.

Fortunately, Mason's coach seemed to be made of the same stuff as much current crush.

You can't have a crush on your kid's summer football trainer. Even if he was the only one who had taken the timeout to listen to both Brady... And me.

Double wince for the desperation bid on the lonely reindeer at the bar.

That was not the right reason to crush on a man. Even a six foot something plus one who looked like Mason that I wanted to lick.

Stop. That.

We need to focus on restaurant things. Not the lick-able football thighs.

Okay, this was getting out of hand. Or thighs. Uh, rugby hormones. Or, something.

I wanted to rest my head in my hands and make

a hideous, unsociably acceptable noise, but instead I kept on smiling until my cheeks ached. Mason's coach looked slightly alarmed.

"Your table is this way," I managed to utter through fixed, straining facial muscles.

My body moved on its own as I rotated on my heel and marched my reindeer dressed behind up the stairs, leading Mason and his coach back to his teammates. By the time I reached the top of the stairs, the fake as hell smile had fallen off my face and my muscles resumed their usual programming.

"Thanks for the guide," Leon muttered. He squished past me and greeted his players to a chorus that grew louder the longer I loitered in a place I no longer needed to be in right now.

"You're welcome." I dithered on a little longer, counting heads and plates, noting the distinct lack of courses that should have arrived but hadn't. I twisted on my behooved boots, the fluffiness of my costume swinging about with me, and ran face first into a solid wall.

Yup, that's what I'd be calling Mason when I was able to breathe again and didn't host a face resembling a reindeer that started with the letter R.

"Are you okay? Sorry about that." Mason poked gingerly at my tenderised nose.

"I'm fine." I batted his hand away and turned about, aiming for the stairs, but he was still in the way. "Uh–" I looked up at him expectantly. And up. *When did he get so damn tall?*

Or maybe I'd just never been quite this close. Picking him up from training with Brady didn't usually involve drooling on my son's coach at quite this close range, even if I often engaged in the activity at a reasonable distance. Not to mention that he'd been the centre of more than one late night fantasy over the past two weeks.

Hello, rugby thighs.

Somewhere behind us, a cheer went up as his teammates did something I was sure hit the *inappropriate* bar. The group had become rowdier in the last hour. Not that it was unexpected in any room this full of cheer so close to Christmas when spirits ran high. Still, Mason didn't seem to take any notice of what his teammates were doing.

"I should get back to my job." I motioned to the stairwell behind him, trying to ignore the additional layer of heat crawling up the inside of my reindeer costume. Destination, my cheeks.

"We never have a chance to talk much when I see you at the field." Mason hasn't moved an inch.

I licked my lips. "Now probably isn't the best time either."

The flush that reached my collar insisted on its upward journey. I resigned myself to my fate as an eternal, red-tinged reindeer. The nose wouldn't be my only glowy feature if the object of my rugby fuelled fantasies didn't let me pass any time soon.

"Then when is?" Mason shifted to one side, exposing my exit strategy, though his habitual easy smile was absent. "Normally Brady's about. This time it's my team. I'd—" He drew a deep breath and stopped.

I broke away from studying the stairwell where a fluorescent light flickered. *Must fix that.* "You'd what?" I asked so softly that I didn't think he could hear me over the music that turned up a notch on cue. Hell, I barely heard myself.

"I'd love to take you out on a date." Nope, still no smile. Mason was dead serious.

I swallowed, unsure if I liked this version of him or not. No, it wasn't that I didn't like this part of him. It was just...

The infamous Mason Hale intensity that didn't usually bother me had come out to play.

And at full strength, up close, his presence was no small thing.

"A date." That should have been a question, not a sentence. Mason scrambled my brain as well as my resolve not to have anyone in my life until Brady was older, if ever. Stuart had screwed up more than just one job. "I haven't dated since..."

"Since you left Brady's dad."

"You figured that out, huh?" Any breath I had left evacuated my lungs, along with my escape plan. *Wait. Why does he assume that Stuart didn't walk out on me?*

Answer: because Mason wasn't like any of the men who had hit on me in the last seven years since I walked away from the most toxic person in my life.

"Yeah. I might have done." He rubbed a hand over his jaw where a five o'clock shadow grew that had no right to look as sexy as it did.

"You're normally clean." I gestured to his face and clamped a hand over my mouth. "Sorry. I have no right."

"No." His inked hand dropped to catch my wrist. "This is what I mean. We never get a chance to have a real conversation. Nyla..." Another cheer went up. He winced. "This isn't my usual environment."

My lips twisted in the parody of a smile. "But it is mine. I need to work, Mason," I said gently, prying his touch away even as my heart ached.

His hand did drop this time and he stepped aside in full, letting me escape down the flickering stairwell. I reached the bottom and jumped the last few steps. My reindeer costume fluttered around the top of my thighs as my logical brain caught up with my night's remaining list of things left to do.

Get the function's meals out before they get out of hand up there.

Check the till and cash drawer. Again.

Because that was annoying me. I was still irritated about the weekend before being out so much and having to fess up to Stuart who had stared at me like I'd grown two heads and not been able to count. Not that he knew how to settle an account for the night in the first place, or how to do the banking, only fund it. Or manage staff effectively, or write a roster for that matter.

The stairwell flickered again as I hit the bottom turn, plunging me into darkness with the kitchen on the other side of the well. Here, even the sounds of the party above and the noisy, over-packed restaurant were muted, the kitchen's heat blocked off by two walls of thick cement.

The fluorescent tube made a feeble effort at a flicker, and died.

Add to list: Fix that damn light.

I closed my eyes, revelling in my moment of relative, stolen peace before the restaurant's chaos resumed. All it would take was four short steps to the corner, shove my way through some of those hideous saloon swinging doors that Stuart and his business partner loved—those ones actually screwed on, thankfully—and everything would be back to normal.

Instead, I stood in my void of muted nothingness and inhaled.

And wasted time that wasn't mine to take.

Why did I push him away?

I pressed the heels of my hands to my eyes, bumping my reindeer antlers back where the headband had slipped forward a touch and blew out a long breath.

"That sounded heartfelt."

Warm fingers closed around my wrists, tugging my hands from where I covered my eyes like a child, hiding away from the world.

Hey, any strategy in a storm.

Only it wasn't a storm I stared into, but Mason Hale's piercing stare. His eyes were darker in the shadowed area as I cowered from a place where, just for one night, I didn't want to be. Here. At all.

Except maybe with him.

CHAPTER SIX

NYLA

The wayward thought fluttered across my mind in a tempting caress, or maybe that was his thumbs brushing back and forth across my pulse points in the ultimate distraction.

"Stop that," I murmured, tugging my hands free, but his fingers closed in a firm circle around my wrists.

"Not just yet." Mason stepped into my space, filling it with everything I'd been aching for in the last weeks.

What I didn't know I had been missing from my life until our lives collided because of my son who loved to kick up dust balls and run amok in all the best ways. But right now, Brady wasn't about to distract either of us.

"Are you stalking me?" I tried for a lighter tone, tugging at his hold still, but both of us knew there was little effort in the motion.

And he didn't let go.

"If that's what it needs to be. I didn't want to let you run away like that. You seemed..." Mason frowned. "I know you've got a job to do, Nyla. Hell, I'm working when I see you too, in the afternoons. It's like we're orbiting around each other's lives, two magnets that bump across each other but never match up. But I'm tired of waiting." The intensity of him ratcheted up to blazing point as he released one wrist.

A cold spot bloomed where he had touched me. The absence of his skin contacting mine left me bereft in an instant. I raised my hand self-consciously. "I want to—" I stared, but stopped when I wasn't sure what, exactly, I wanted.

It didn't matter, because Mason filled in the blanks for me.

His free hand scooped through my hair where it hung down my back like a heated curtain, cupping my nape. Long, strong fingers latched across my jaw, angling my head back. He gave me a fraction of a second to object, but either my head didn't like playing catch up tonight, or—

I didn't want to object to anything he offered.

His mouth crashed down onto mine, his kiss hard and possessive. A tiny sound I couldn't prevent slipped from my lips that might have been a sigh, or surrender. I didn't have a clue. All I knew was the moment before he kissed me, those dark eyes of his filled my world, full of blazing intensity. And then I didn't think at all.

Because I didn't have to.

My body took over, knowing exactly what it wanted from this man who had featured in plenty of my filthy one a.m. fantasies when I couldn't sleep and needed to keep my panic attacks at bay.

I leaned back against the wall behind me, rising onto my toes to reach him. My heels did little to negate the height difference between my five foot, five inches and the giant towering over me. Not that it seemed to bother him. Mason growled against my mouth, flicking his tongue across the seam of my lips impatiently. I gasped at the sensation as he surged forward.

His tongue pushed into my mouth as his knee nudged between my legs. I moaned at the dual sensation, unprepared for the overwhelm that left me shaking in his arms after so little contact from anyone for so long. *Starved for affection?* But he removed my ability to think with every touch, and I was grateful for that. Mason released my other wrist to sink his fingers into my hip, squeezing roughly.

The second sound that tore from my lips froze me in place as my mind slammed into gear. I leaned back but he came with me, his kisses insistent, unceasing. The taste of him, the peat whiskey he'd been drinking, paired with something sweeter, rolled through me. I knew I'd associate that scent with him forever. My hands slid up his chest and with the last remnant of my willpower, I drew everything I had left behind a single effort and *pushed*.

Mason didn't so much as budge, but he did lean back a bare inch, breaking this kiss that left me somewhere in No Reindeer Land, my lips halfway between bruised and tingling. I hated how much I loved that sensation and craved more of it.

"Am I hurting you?" he asked, his brow dipping as he searched my face. The hand at my hip softened a touch, but he didn't let me go. "Nyla? What did I do?"

I didn't realise I was panting until I tried to etch a word out. "You– I– Here–" I closed my mouth and tried to make a full sentence like a proper grown up.

It took me two more tries and bless, Mason must've had the patience of a reindeer patron saint to deal with me right then. "I can't do this. Not here. Please," my voice cracked on that last word.

The pressure of his fingers on my hip lessened as he eased back a step. "Alright."

"Okay." *This is too easy.* Or just wrong.

The moment Mason stepped back, releasing his grip on my neck, I could breathe and think clearly again.

Part of me wanted to scream for him to come back, but I pushed him away and I couldn't rescind that. Because what I'd said was true. We couldn't do this here. Intimacy. Anything resembling a personal moment more than the precious seconds we just stole.

Not with the chance of his teammates or coach, who frankly scared all hell out of me, walking back down those stairs at any moment. Or one of my girls, or worse, coming through the swinging doors.

And if I just shattered the only moment I'll ever have with him?

My heart cramped in my chest at the thought, the smoky/sweet taste of him lingering on my tongue. I raised my fingers to my still tingling lips. His narrowed gaze locked in on the movement.

"Are you gonna let me take you somewhere so we can...keep talking?"

A twisted laugh bubbled in my throat that I managed to keep to myself lest I paint a picture of an insane reindeer before him. "Talking? That's what we're calling this?" I hissed, pointing a crooked finger between us.

Mason's slow smile was beyond devastating. "Gorgeous, you can call it whatever the hell you want, as long as you promise me that's not the last time I'll taste that mouth...or other parts of you." His gaze took a lazy survey of my body that overheated on demand.

My reindeer persona melted on the spot.

"I'm just going to take Rudolph for a walk before I need to change," I muttered, fanning myself to his booming laughter. *So much for keeping a stolen moment to ourselves.* "You are not out of trouble, Mason Hale."

"I wouldn't have it any other way, Nyla." The way my name rolled off his tongue left me shivery and hot all at once.

I slipped out of the dark space as the fluorescent light bulb made a desperate dash for life. It flickered too brightly right as I sneaked into the kitchen to find Chaz giving me a thumbs up.

Brady's flushed face stared up at me from the dish-washing station where he wore an oversized t-shirt that far from fitted his slim frame. A bright smile split his face.

The fluorescent bar behind me glowed like the sun. Too bright—as every light in the kitchen seemed to follow suit, before the entire restaurant plunged into darkness.

I covered my face in my hands, and let out a small wail as the music died as well. Apparently, the front of the house ran on the same fuse, or the box had blown entirely. Who knew?

"Myla, power's out," Captain Obvious—probably Josie—called from what sounded like the bar.

"Fucking brilliant," I muttered into my hands, hoping my words came out muffled.

From the snicker that came from one of the tables near the kitchen at my back, apparently my hands didn't muffle shit.

Nor did the silence do a damn thing for the volume of my overly enthusiastic son who chose that moment to yell at the top of his lungs, "Hey, Mum! Did you kiss Mason Hale?"

Cue more restaurant general hilarity and my freshly reinstated Rudolph status. Chaz flicked on his phone flashlight app that nearly blinded me as I raised my face to find him still giving me a thumbs up.

The smile slid off his face as I pivoted on my heel to deal with whatever stood behind me.

Please be Mason. Please be Mason.

But I knew even as I turned around from the overpowering, atrociously super sweet aftershave that accosted me that it wasn't the male specimen that I hoped for.

Stuart glowered at me as I faced off with him in a stale, silent moment. Then he jerked his head toward the door at the back of the kitchen. "Outside. You can fix this."

I didn't know if he meant the blacked out restaurant, my drooping reindeer costume or my untimely kiss with a rugby star on his premises. Nor did I really want to find out. But he was still technically my employer, as well as my ex, so I followed him through the kitchen in a walk of shame, my antlers held as high as my costume allowed while Chaz cheered quietly for me.

Welp, at least I had someone's support. Tonight, I'd take that with both hands. Hooves, even.

I even managed not to let the door hit me on my tailpiece on the way out.

CHAPTER SEVEN

MASON

I *shouldn't have kissed her.*

Nothing else crossed my mind as the lights went out and the restaurant plunged into darkness. I took the steps in pairs—or maybe threes—hearing Coach's voice berating me in the back of my head about busted ankles before next season even started and the upcoming charity match, but paid his grumpy ass voice no attention anyway.

All I wanted was to get to Nyla because I couldn't leave her like that. Flushed and jittering about like a glow bug on New Year's with nowhere to go. But when I hit the darkened kitchen in time to hear Brady's too-loud comment in the silence, I knew I was in the wrong place at the wrong time.

Or maybe at the right time.

And then her ex talked down to her like she was nothing.

Fuck me. I'll rip that man apart.

Torn between letting her look after herself and standing square between her and the asshole she shouldn't have to deal with anymore, I hesitated a second too long. When I reached for her again, my swiping hand came up empty. A second later, the lights flickered back on, and I stood in a kitchen full of cooks all staring at me, wearing identical grins on their faces.

A tug at hip height broke the uncomfortable silence.

"Brady. Uh, hi." I cleaned my throat as he motioned me down to him. Hell, I swore this kid grew taller every time I saw him.

"Mason." Brady cupped his hands around his mouth and yelled into my ear.

I winced. "Yeah, mate."

"You kissed my mum."

I'd be deaf by the end of the night, and it had nothing to do with the extra whiskey chaser I threw back with Leon earlier.

"Yeah, mate."

Brady giggled. "Are you gonna come stay with us? She doesn't date, you know that."

"Yeah, I—" *Shit, which question am I answering?* I cleared my throat and stretched my cramped calves. "I know she doesn't date, mate. We're gonna take it slow, okay? Look after you both. Cause you're important."

Brady's face fell a bit and I felt like shit on the spot. "Okay."

I ruffled his hair. "It's gonna be okay, bud." I wanted to tack on an *I promise* at the end of that, but I couldn't commit to that without speaking to Nyla first, so I didn't. The breath I let out said everything I felt, so I left it at that. The little dude at my waist height seemed to get it, thankfully. He'd seen more than his fair share of fights, I figured, from how his dad and their relationship seemed to progress, shitty as that hand had dealt out to him.

But as I raised my head to face off with the rest of the kitchen, thankfully only one cook was left staring at me. He offered a double thumbs up and jerked his head toward the back door I hadn't noticed before.

"She's out there with St–" Brady took a deep breath and tried again. "With Stuart." He shuffled on the spot.

"You think they're fighting?" I looked down at him, recalling the bruises on Nyla's wrist when I first met her. I'd never asked where they came from, but if he hurt her, Leon would have a hell of a media storm to clean up in the aftermath. My jaw tightened.

There were a lot of questions I wanted to ask that I couldn't because he was nine, and that wasn't fair on him. Nor could I ask the chef guy, because the kitchen was full of people all pretending not to listen in about Nyla's private life where I got the impression they already knew plenty.

The supportive chef guy opened his mouth as I headed for the door, but it wasn't his hand on my arm that stopped me.

"Leave it." Leon's command halted my feet in their tracks, my body preprogrammed to respond to his commands.

I sighed and stared down at the floor. A pair of my smaller shoes joined mine. I ignored my coach for a long moment. "Does your dad ever hurt your mum, Brady?" I asked in a tight voice I couldn't shake.

So much for not letting the kitchen staff in on her private life.

He shrugged. "They just fight when they're

together. A lot." His soggy looking trainers shuffled about on the floor leaving dirty marks that the cook guy would have to clean up later if Brady didn't. "And I don't call him dad."

"Yeah, I got that." I ruffled his hair with my hand. "If there's trouble, I'm right upstairs, alright?" I kept my eyes on Brady, but I'd said that last loud statement enough for the entire kitchen to hear because, fuck it. If they were nosy enough to eavesdrop in on the conversation, they could damn well keep an eye on our girl too.

Because she was my girl, and nothing in this world would change that. Not after the way she kissed me back a few minutes ago.

"You're on."

Unsurprisingly, the chef guy answered me.

I gave him a tight nod and followed Leon back upstairs to join the rest of my team. I had a party to fake it for the rest of the night. Hell, if Nyla was gonna be alright, I might even join them.

"Another two sets and you're done," Leon called from the bottom of the stairs while my thighs screamed at me.

I'll never skip leg day ever again. I'll never skip leg day again.

I repeated the mantra over again in my head as I powered through the third to last flight in the stair climb challenge, trying not to count the rows in the stadium that I still had to go to, knowing that Leon was full of shit. He had a bad habit of adding an extra set of reps onto whatever training we were on. Today would be no different, even if it was a solo run.

I'll never skip leg day...

I would have bitched at him aloud if I didn't think I'd earn myself another double set of reps and a whole lot of cussing—if I had the breath to spare. Instead, I threw that energy into working through a hell of a hangover cure for drinking too much the night before with the team in a rare effort to match them one after I watched Nyla walk back into the restaurant and push her ex away when he tried to manhandle her.

She hadn't let me or anyone else near her for the rest of the night, but one of the girls slipped me her number—that I already had from her contact form for Brady's summer coaching clinic, though I'd never used it, not being for the right reasons. But this felt different.

The moment I walked out of the themed restaurant and she was out of my sight, I lit her phone up, figuring she'd answer me if she had time, if I was lucky, or the other side of never if I wasn't, and I'd be begging her on my knees with an apology today.

If my knees would take it.

But she hadn't left me hanging after all.

MASON: Good to see the asshole left you alone. Brady gave me some pointers.

MASON: I'm still gonna ask you out on that date.

MASON: Let me know if you get home safe after work? Not stalking. Just looking out for you.

I left it after that, pocketing my phone as I walked along the main street with the team who sang their favourite rugby rock anthems—badly—at the top of their lungs. Hell, after a few rounds, I started to join them, until my pocket vibrated enough to break through my whiskey and beer induced haze.

NYLA: Please tell me that's not you singing.

NYLA: OMFG. It is you singing. I can tell.

NYLA: Stuart isn't a worry. He's just frustrating. But thank you.

I watched the dots come and go after that last message for long enough that the team walked on without me. I dropped back, my feet half turned in the direction of the restaurant when her last message finally came through.

NYLA: I'll hold you to that date sometime. Life is kinda crazy right now but... sometime.

MASON: Sometime works for me. See you at the Granny Grapple in the morning. 🤍

My thumbs fumbled the keypad in my haste to spell out a reasonable reply. I had no idea what the various coloured hearts meant, but the purple one suited her in my head, so that's what I sent. She hearted the message after a moment, but didn't reply and I figured I wasn't in too much shit.

Pocketing my phone, I jogged after the team, wrapping my arm around someone's neck and let myself be drawn into the next pub along the street. The boys drank and made merry. Hell, after a few I joined them while Leon leaned back and watched us get tanked.

That had been an easy decision at ten p.m. the night before. Now, with the sparrows not quite farting just after sunrise and every muscle straining while I sweated myself stupid before the charity event on the last day of the summer training clinic, I ran stair after stair after stair until I knew I'd dream of the things.

Finally I collapsed at the end of the third set—*called it*—at Coach's feet. "Fuck, you're cruel," I gasped, reaching for my water.

He raised an eyebrow. "You thought getting pissed last night was smart just because you kissed a pretty girl and she agreed to go out on a date with your sorry ass?"

I groaned out loud and rolled over, glad I didn't have the urge to puke my guts up into the grass I laid on. "What, you're fucking psychic now too? Perfect. I can't keep a damn secret from you or any of my family. Just come round for lunch, man. You and my aunties can all gossip like bitches together."

"What did you just call me?"

I stared up at Leon and shut my mouth.

"Smart move, Hale. Get your ass up and shower. You have a Granny Grapple to host in less than two hours. Ice bath will be waiting for you. Recover fast, kid."

A groan left me as I tipped my head back and starfished on the grass, letting my eyes slam shut. "Yeah, fuck. I forgot about that."

Two and a bit hours later, it wasn't only my thighs that stung like all get out. The grannies lined up and Coach shook his collection bucket like a pro. The man had donned his tiniest tighty-whities for the honour, and shook that too, I swore.

The biddies lined up for the privilege of dropping in their gold coins and change into his bucket and tackling me plus getting their media picture taken afterward. I braced myself as the next Blue Rinse charged forward, rocking me back onto my heels. Together we tumbled onto the thick mat that I swore had my butt permanently imprinted onto it.

I helped Blue Rinse up and knelt for the obligatory picture afterward, wincing twice over as she went in for the bum grab.

Brady waved from the stands while Nyla laughed at me behind her hand. I'd spent forty-five hellish minutes running up and down those this morning at daybreak, and they weren't my favourite thing, but she sure as hell was. I waved back, refraining from rubbing my injured behind and deflated my ego as my phone buzzed and the most recent granny released my butt.

NYLA: *Brady says you should keep falling over and that you're doing a great job.*

I shook my head and gave a mock thumbs down as I glanced up at them. Nyla laughed at me outright.

"Smile," Leon muttered, shaking his bucket and his tush for all he was worth.

A very much *not* Granny threw a fifty into the bucket and gave me a too-white bright smile as she lined up to grapple me.

"Hey, that's not fair," I protested, glancing up at the stands and back at Leon. Coach just shrugged, but Nyla's smile disappeared on cue.

"She's paid." Leon's professional *suck-it-up* face was back in place. "Make it count."

I braced my burning thighs and took the fall, rolling out from under the groping arms as soon as I could free myself and smiled vaguely for the camera. But by the time I freed myself from Miss Very Much Not a Granny, the stands had thinned out and Nyla and Brady were nowhere in sight.

I fished my phone out of my pocket, hoping for a snarky message, but there was none waiting.

> MASON: Are you still around? I was hoping we could do something after. I'm good with Brady around if you are.

I waited for her response, but unlike the other night at the restaurant, Nyla wasn't in a chatty mood. I sighed and pocketed my phone, helping Leon pack up after he completed his end of season Coach's speech, said a few words to my remaining kids and their parents and headed home.

To a family that would smother me and a full house that included everyone but the two people I wanted to spend the rest of my day with the most.

CHAPTER EIGHT

NYLA

The moment Mason took his last tackle of the charity day, my phone rang. I picked the call up without looking, and wished I hadn't.

"Get back to the restaurant," Stuart snapped into my ear without offering a greeting. "You need to fix these accounts now."

I sighed and ran my hand through my hair, motioning for Brady to stay where he sat and turned away, keeping my voice low. "I know there's money missing, Stuart. I just need time to work out who it is, and why."

"Oh, that's cute. Like you know who it isn't." His voice grew cold.

My blood matched his tone. "Excuse me?"

"You know what I mean, Nyla. You. Chasing after that football player. Climbing all over him here. It's pathetic, just like you. If you're that broke, just ask me for help. I'll give you money if you need it, for fuck's sake. Come by the restaurant and I'll give you cash. Just...tell me what I need to do with these accounts so I can fix them with the bank, and—"

"Stuart," I interrupted him, my voice remarkably steady for the amount of bullshit that just spewed my way. "Did you just accuse me outright of stealing from your business?"

He had the good sense not to speak for a moment. "Well, I thought you—"

"Good. because that's what I thought you said. And all I have to say to you are two words. Please listen carefully. Fuck. Off."

I pressed the *END* button gently on my phone and slid it into my bag that hung from my shoulder. A shuddering breath left me, but the visceral response I expected didn't come. Maybe because this was Stuart, and I was all too used to his rubbish after so many years. I breathed in a long, slow breath and turned back to find my son watching me with a distinct expression of awe and something akin to pride decorating his young face.

"Go, Mum," he said in a soft voice for once.

"You heard that, huh?" I bit my lip. *Damn.* I thought I'd been more discreet.

Brady nodded. "Your part. It's not so hard to guess that Stuart is being an asshole again."

"You shouldn't use language like that." I held my hand out to him.

His face fell. "Sorry. Can't we stay?"

I glanced down at the grounds to where Mason's coach was starting his wrap up talk for the end of the charity event. "I think they're finishing off. You know we're going to catch up with Mason another time, right?" I added in casually.

"Yeah, I guessed you were going to keep snogging. St– Dad's going to hate that." Brady grinned at me.

"Right." I coughed into my palm and headed toward the parking lot. "Come on. Let's get you some lunch, huh? What do you want?" My stomach cramped down on nothing at all. I'd only be feeding Brady because I'd essentially just walked out on the only job I had. And while there were some savings in my bank account, with monthly rent and bills that wouldn't last long. It looked like I'd be job hunting from this afternoon onwards. I didn't want to worry Brady, and so lunch for him it would be.

I climbed into my car, willing myself not to look

back for Mason or check my phone for his messages. There would more than likely be a stack from Stuart, and I didn't want to have to deal with those anyway, so it was easier to ignore everyone for a bit.

My blood was still icy from Stuart's oh-so-simple accusation of theft as I bought Brady drive through and spoiled myself with a steaming hot coffee. I'd regret that splurge later, I knew, but right now I needed that fortifying hot drink as I drove back toward the restaurant. Another choice I hated, but Chaz was on evening prep and I could leave Brady downstairs safely with him while I sorted this out with Stuart once and for all.

Because there was no way in hell that I wanted him spreading rumours that I stole from the restaurant, or else I'd never get another job at all.

I pulled up in my little rust bucket of a buzz box car and parked beside Stuart's shiny secondary midlife crisis divorce present to himself. The first being the stripper he cheated on me with while I was still breastfeeding our son. Brady grabbed a fidget toy from the glove compartment and twisted the spiral coil around his wrist over and over in a dizzying pattern as we walked in through the back of the restaurant that had all its lights on, thankfully.

Fixing the fuse the night before hadn't been a

hard job at all. Dealing with Stuart of course, took longer. I poked my head into the cool room and found Chaz belting out the lyrics to *Phantom of the Opera* to himself—both parts—with a remarkable degree of talent.

I grinned and pointed to Brady. "Can you two keep each other company for a bit? I need to have a chat with the guy upstairs."

A grimace crossed his face at the mention of Stuart. "Of course. For you, anything." Chaz frowned as he stared at my shaking coffee cup. Some of the hot liquid dripped over the side onto my hand, but I could barely feel it. "Nyla. What has he done to you?"

I shrugged. "Accused me of taking the top off the till and that's why we're short, and because he hates that I'm with Mason, and have my own life, and that I'm broke. Oh, and now jobless. The usual, I'm sure." I pushed the words out as though they meant nothing, despite that we both knew that they did.

Chaz held his silence as I left his kitchen. I missed his rambunctious singing almost immediately as I started up the stairwell that remained brightly lit the whole way up. *At least something is working.* I sighed and patted the wall. *My last time.* The promise I made to myself. I waited for the tears to start, and wondered when I would feel anything at all but... I didn't.

Nothing. It didn't matter. But it should. Maybe I was numb. I spent more hours within these four walls than I did at home or anywhere else. How many times in the last two weeks had I dropped Brady at football in order to dart back here to complete a shift because someone else hadn't turned up? I'd left Josie at the till, minding the front door, pulling her off the bar when no one else was around...

When no one else was around to see what she took.

I closed my eyes. "Fuck," I whispered softly to myself. "Opportunity."

One of the main ways theft occurred. And worse, an opportunity that I had created because I was too busy in my own life to notice the gap I created.

Damnit, this was my fault.

"Stuart." I jogged the last few steps into the upper level that housed the event space along with the office and the private shower with its change room built off the side. "I know what's happening with the accounts. Let me show you before I leave." I ran out of breath on that last one, *knowing* I shouldn't be here but just like when I kicked him out last time, I needed closure.

Which was why I still fought with him, why I still didn't walk away, and why I let him have time with Brady even though our son—questionable language choices aside—got it right. Stuart was an asshole. He proved that with his shitty line this afternoon about the theft when he *knew* it wasn't me, but this was my banking and credit rating as well as his that was getting screwed into the ground if he let it run on. And work out a way to talk to Josie because maybe she was a woman in a situation, like mine before I left Suart, that I could help her avoid. I hoped.

Plus, I needed to clear the air.

Air that moaned right as I stepped up onto the mezzanine level. The sound zipped around me. I froze in place, though after a moment my feet kept travelling forward because I had to *know*, even though I should have turned around and trounced my behind right back down those stairs and stayed right out of my ex's restaurant forever. Because we had been here before. Maybe not in this space, but the last time I found him with another woman.

The moans continued, growing louder as I turned the corner to face the open end of the office. Right to where Stuart had set up his office chair that he rarely sat in, unless he was drinking on premises.

Josie was splayed across his lap, her legs spread wide open so I could see right up underneath her far-too-short-for-work skirt and apron, to where his hand disappeared inside her.

Her head was thrown back onto my ex's shoulder. She writhed for him in what had to be the best fakest orgasm of her life because both she and I shared a singular truth in that moment:

Stuart wasn't that good.

Not with any part of his anatomy.

Tongue, hands or dick. It didn't matter. You couldn't pay that man to learn how to use anything. He was beyond a selfish lover. Which told me two things straight up.

He knew who was pulling money out of the till before he called me with his little shame charade earlier knowing I'd offer to help him with the cash and banking because I was just that predictable, and...

That this little show was for my benefit alone.

The rage that hasn't hit me before fuelled my veins now. I stared straight into Stuart's emotionless, dead eyes as Josie reached the peak of her performance and smiled.

"She's full of shit, Stuart. I won't be back."

I turned around, walked steadily down the stairs,

gave Chaz the best hug I could offer as Josie started to rant and rage above us to whatever bullshit Stuart didn't offer her, collected my son, and drove away without mangling my ex's car, but damn was it a close thing. Not that any of it mattered.

He thought he'd had his revenge. That backfired on him. I got what I wanted when I walked into that office. I found my closure, and I walked out with my son.

Hell, I could even splurge on a milkshake after that. While Brady downed his treat in record time despite having eaten lunch earlier—hello, hollow growing boy stomach—I sent out the message that was long overdue. I prayed I didn't send it too late.

NYLA: Can I still collect on that date?

CHAPTER NINE

MASON

I stood near the entrance to the car park of *Old Man Han's* pub and tried not to jiggle on my feet. Sure, I was fifteen minutes early for the time that I'd agreed on with Nyla a week earlier, but there was no way in hell did I have any intention of being late on the date it took me weeks to get with her.

I flipped my phone in my hand and pocketed it half a dozen times, stepping back out of the way of the line that formed around the corner to the main entrance. Even early in the night, the pub, a hot spot in its own right, built up a vibe that said the place should be packed. But tonight, inside, it would be a decent date night for Nyla and me. Assuming I got the time right and hadn't screwed up.

Finally, her little car turned into the driveway. She gave me a harried wave through the window, the tiny wheels bumping over the gravel as she pulled in and parked next to my truck. The Ute was my favourite thing in the world. I kept it white and spotless. The tiniest bit of dust usually bothered all hell out of me, but not tonight.

I grinned broadly as Nyla slammed her car door and trotted over to me, slinging a teensy beaded bag that couldn't possibly hold anything important over her shoulder. Her long black hair swung in a silky black sheet to below her ass, the sheen melding with a floor length black skirt with a slit up the side that sat snug on her waist.

A thin strip of golden skin was visible at her stomach, the slightest curve there leaving my hands aching to palm her against me, before a strapless top of the matching material, also beaded, started.

In my simple black shirt and jeans I might have felt under dressed next to her but... She just blew me away and I couldn't stop staring.

"You look beautiful," I murmured over a lump that developed in my throat and refused to budge.

She stopped at my side, panting a little and threw her hair over her shoulder. "I'm sorry. I didn't mean to be late. The babysitter isn't one I've used before. I couldn't get my regular. Brady wasn't sure about her, said he'd seen her with Stuart, and I didn't want to leave him, so I left him at my sister-in-law, who isn't the easiest person, and—"

"Hey. It's okay." I cupped her hip without thinking, leaning down to kiss the corner of her mouth. She stopped talking and stared at me. "Brady comes first, always. You're second but only by a fraction, okay? Tonight is about you."

"Oh." Her hand drifted lightly over the back of my knuckles but she didn't push my touch away.

Thank Christ, because I wouldn't have known what the hell to do with myself if she did.

"Come inside with me? I booked a table." I broke contact with her waist. The warmth of her still seared into my palm as I offered her my hand.

Nyla looked up at me with a tentative question in her eyes that said everything all at once. And, knowing something of her history, I promised myself I'd try not to be the asshole like the ex who'd hurt her so badly that she hadn't let herself date for the last ten years or however long since the catastrophe of him in her life.

"Alright," she said softly, slipping her hand into mine, giving me a fraction of her trust.

I held onto her firmly, and headed back through

the parking lot. Nyla hesitated, and I tugged on her hand. "Secret entrance." I grinned. "You want to avoid the crowd?" I raised an eyebrow, nodding in the direction of the line that wound halfway around the block and across the next street.

She stared. "Won't inside be packed?"

I shrugged. "Like I said, I booked a table."

"Uh huh." Her eyes narrowed a little, and I swore she was about to start hissing at me. Mind, the pissed off kitten look was sexy as all fuck on her, so I wasn't complaining.

Still grinning like a loon, I led Nyla in through the staff entrance at the back of the pub. The kitchen staff greeted us with raised hands at the food prep station. I checked over my shoulder to make sure my girl wasn't freaking out, but she looked around the area with interest. One girl raised a hand to wave, and Nyla waved back. I huffed a laugh under my breath. Typical industry—everyone knew everyone.

I stepped out onto the main floor and found the man I searched for waiting for me behind the bar. "Hansen."

"My man." The giant of the Sanford Sentinels stepped out around the bar and slung one arm around my shoulders. He was the only player on the team who matched me in height, but by far over-whelmed me in terms of bulk. "And this is..." he trailed off and let me do the honours.

"Nyla. This is my teammate and mentor, Hansen Beaucliff. He's our forward prop. He does the heavy work in the scrums," I explained when Nyla shook her head.

"It's nice to meet you." She looked around the nearly empty room, apart from a few select dinners and back to us. "Shouldn't— shouldn't this place be packed? There's a line outside..." she faltered off when Hansen laughed, and looked down.

"Don't do that," I said softly. "You don't have to hide here. Nyla runs a restaurant on the other side of town. Cowboy's Pitstop."

"Does she?" Hansen eyed her with interest.

"I used to," Nyla said softly, raising her head with no small amount of defiance glittering in her stun-ning eyes. "I quit last week when my ex—my boss," she corrected herself, "accused me of theft, then set up the staff member who did to um..." she waved a hand vaguely and turned pink.

Hansen's eyebrows shot for the ceiling. "Sounds like a damn good reason to quit to me," he muttered. "Yes, we have a line around the block. We close for...

certain arrangements. Jenna will show you to your table." He shot me a hard look and turned back to the bar, muttering under his breath about shit business owners who didn't look after their staff, not keeping his voice half as low as he should have, or maybe that was the point.

A girl dressed in a long sleeved white shirt and black pressed slacks with her hair pulled back in a ponytail smiled at Nyla. "This way."

Nyla blinked. "I expected you to talk to him." She looked back at me.

The server, Jenna, wrinkled her nose. "I'm pretty sure he gets enough attention, don't you?" She winked and turned around to lead us to a table set off to one corner.

Red wood planking created a semi booth that hid us from the rest of the mostly empty restaurant where Hansen had allowed just enough patrons in for this part of the night to create a cozy ambience without letting the place feel bare or empty. A mini coach lantern glowed softly above us as Nyla slid into one side. I sneaked into the L-shape beside her.

"This is really nice, Mason. Thank you. He's mad not for letting the rest of those people in, though. Losing a ton of cash."

"Yeah, it'll cost me a few favours, for sure." I snapped my mouth shut, but the words slipped out.

Nyla's head turned as what I said sank in. "Are you shitting me?"

I winced. "No?" I sighed. "It can get hectic, with the media. Some nights it's normal. Some nights...it's not so normal. I wanted to take you somewhere nice without it being fussy and...this is the best place I know. Apart from my aunt's cooking, but don't let my mother know that. She'll skin me."

Her nose twitched. "Okay, so you might have dug yourself out of that one. Saved by the aunt I'll never meet. But seriously." Nyla twisted in her seat, peeking around me at the door. "Hansen shouldn't close up just to give us–"- she jabbed an elbow lightly at my midsection, "or *you* privacy or favours. It's kinda sweet and weird at once."

"He has this place because he loves it. Loves working, and always wanted a pub of his own. Not for money, Nyla. We've all got enough of that to keep us going for years. Some of us just love to work."

She scoffed. "Yeah, because you ran the summer clinic for pocket change."

"Actually, I donated it all to the Granny Challenge. It goes to a dementia secure ward because there was a fire in a local one. That's why Leon and I set up the clinic in the first place. Not everything is about money, Nyla. We don't all have the fucked up motivations like your ex." I reached out to touch her cheek and found her skin burning.

Fuck.

"Okay." She tipped her head away, but I couldn't leave it like that.

"I keep fucking up with you, don't I?" I stroked my fingers across her cheek until she looked at me, and my heart fucking shattered at the pain reflected in her eyes. I didn't need to ask *who hurt you* because I knew already. Him—and now, maybe even me. "I'm sorry," I said softly, still stroking her cheek. "I'm gonna try not to shove what I think down your throat from now on, okay?"

She laughed and leaned into my touch. "That's actually okay. I like that you believe in *something* that you're passionate about, even if your view of the world is a bit skewed. Not all of us have that sort of... Privilege."

My lips twisted into a grin. "If I told you that I grew up on an island with less than three hundred people on it, and dinner came from my tiny back-yard, including the animals I named as a kid, would that change things?" I flipped open a menu before she could answer.

Nyla blinked at me. "Perspective, huh?"

I nodded slowly. "Yeah. I could do with a bit of that."

"No, I mean me. Drink?" She smiled shyly at me, lacing our fingers together in a knot I wasn't sure I'd be able to undo if I had to, and wasn't sure I wanted to break anyway.

The date went smoothly from there. A guy with a guitar introduced himself on the stage by the bar and started playing. I forgot his name as I listened to Nyla talk about herself and Brady, tucking away each tiny fragment of information she offered, stilted at first then gaining confidence when I never shot her down like I suspected the assholic ex must have done whenever she opened her mouth.

By the time the last morsel of our shared chocolate mousse and fancy cream that I couldn't pronounce, but she did, was gone, she'd let me slide my arm across her shoulders, and snuggled into my side. Hansen had opened the doors half an hour before and turned the sound up on the guitarist who played slightly fast rock covers. I pressed my lips to the top of her head and inhaled.

"Frangipanis."

"What?" Nyla looked up at me dozily. "I think I've been food coma-ed."

"You smell like frangipanis." I inhaled a long, slow breath again. *Smells like home.* "Maybe marsh-mallows or something sweet."

She giggled, batting at me. "I think you're analysing my shampoo. Or my moisturiser. Or something."

"I like it."

"Um, good?" She smiled up at me, finishing the sparkling lime water she'd requested earlier, refusing alcohol.

I got the impression Stuart was responsible for that, too, and promised myself that if we ever crossed paths again, there would be words. I still wasn't sure what happened, exactly, that day she quit the restaurant, and I didn't want to push her, but it had to be bad from the way rebellion rolled from her in waves when she talked about it earlier. Which also meant she was jobless. I turned that thought over in my head, and hated that I'd brought up money earlier. One of my aunts reached out and distance slapped me for my thoughtlessness.

Pushing the thought to the back of my mind for now, I tangled my fingers in her hair and tugged gently. "How long have you got the babysitter for, gorgeous?"

A small tremor rippled through her fine frame. "All night?"

She made it a question, but there wasn't one in her jet gaze when her eyes locked on mine.

"Good." I leaned down and pressed my lip to her temple. "Can I drive you home? Your car is safe here overnight. Hansen lives above the bar. And his Lexus is parked right below the back door."

She nodded, her knotted fingers squeezing mine as that fine full-body tremor repeated itself. Jenna appeared on cue with the bill. I signed for it before Nyla could offer to pay. She huffed at me, but didn't fight when I tipped her chin up and pressed my lips lightly to hers in a brief kiss that tested my control.

"Let me have this, okay? One night where I get to spoil you. Then you can go back to sassing all hell out of me after midnight."

Her eyes sparkled at me beneath the coach lantern swaying above us in time with the music. "You promise?"

"With everything I am." I led her between the full tables, back out the way we came, waving to Hansen over my shoulder.

He waved back. "See you at the exhibition match next week."

I groaned. "Hell. I forgot about that."

"Coach won't let you. Get your beauty sleep." He winked at Nyla. "Don't let him push you around."

"Never." She broke away from me to reach up and give the giant of a man a huge hug, whispering something I couldn't hear over the crowd's growing chatter.

I stared down at her in wonder as she bounced back alongside me. "What was that?"

She shrugged. "I told him his steaks were a thousand percent better than the Cowboy's Pitstop ones, and that there's also a chef he needs to headhunt called Chaz who is totally underutilized there."

I stared at her for a long moment, then laughed. "You are the sweetest damn thing, you know that?" I found her hand again. "Most people find him scary as hell."

"I think they say that about you, too."

I stopped, holding the back door of the pub open for her after we waved goodbye to the staff and thanked them for our meal. "Really? Me?" I was just the island kid who got a good run, a lucky streak a few years back and managed to hold onto it because of a good team, a better trainer and hard work.

Nyla huffed up at me. "You have no idea, do you? That's who you are, Mason Hale. You're untouchable. The kid who runs faster than anyone, who works the hardest to prove who he is. Arrives before anyone else, trains later and has some of the most unbelievable stats for the season. And you're 'broody looking as hell'." She air quoted me.

From where, I had no idea.

I looked at her askance as I unlocked my truck and held the door for her while she climbed up. "All that, huh?"

"My son might be a fan."

"And you?"

The silky black material of her skirt slipped to expose her thigh. I gathered the soft black fabric in my fist, letting her feel the pull and leaned down and kissed her before she could answer me. Not too rough, but hard enough. Her hand closed over mine and moved it higher along her thigh.

"Maybe. My place is empty tonight. Brady's staying at my sister-in-law's with the sitter." Her mouth opened sweetly beneath mine.

It took every inch of my restraint not to push her back in the leather seat, slide my hand between her legs and find out how fast I could make her come for me in the parking lot right there.

Instead, I backed up, released my hold on her skirt and her thigh that trembled as I let her go, and kissed her gently once more. "Will you give me directions, gorgeous? Because I'm distracted as hell right now."

She nodded as I shut the door, heading around to my side, adjusting my cock in my pants and prayed I'd get us safely across town.

CHAPTER TEN

NYLA

My key had never not fit on my lock so many times in the seven years Brady and I lived in my rented townhouse. That might have had something to do with the rugby player currently kissing his way along my neck, but I was determined to make that key fit and Open. My. Damn. *Door.*

Mason's hands clasped my waist as I rallied my final attempt and aimed my scratched little key at the lock.

And missed.

His lips moved to the hollow of my throat where he sucked gently. A soft *clank* announced my key hitting the cement doorstep at my toes.

"Bugger," I muttered, leaning my head back onto his shoulder.

"Forget it." Mason squeezed my waist rhythmically.

"Forget...what?" Hell, I swore this man's hands were made for sex. Or me. Or...something. I could barely think around him, let alone string a sentence together. "The key? I think we need to get inside, Mace."

He laughed against my skin. "Fuck that." He pushed me to one side, into a tiny nook—read beyond teensy space that hid absolutely nothing—until my back pressed into the alcove that stood perpendicular to the doorway. I stared down the roadway at oncoming cars and their overly strong headlights as I hid in the shadows and Mason dropped to his knees before me.

"What?" Warm, large hands drifted inside my black silk skirt, his calloused fingers pressing my thighs apart. "No, Mason—"

"Hush, Nyla. Or don't. Your neighbourhood could probably do with a show."

Dark eyes glittered in the reflected streetlight, before he dipped his head and licked along the sheer lace of my thong that I opted to wear under my skirt for my date tonight.

My breath hitched, and the noise that followed, slipping from my lips, terrified me. I clamped both hands over my mouth as my thighs trembled, barely holding me up, even though I had the sense that Mason had barely started on whatever he planned for tonight.

One hand pressed to my stomach, pinning me back to the wall, preventing me from sliding down into a Nyla shaped puddle, which is exactly what would have happened if he hadn't caught me before his tongue went back to its devious work. His other fingers stroked lightly across the soft lace, over my aching, slicked flesh.

I moaned into my cupped hands as he tasted me, licking my thighs, making a mess. Deft fingers caught the edge of my sheer thong and flicked the thin material aside. His tongue slid across my waxed skin as I arched against the hand that pinned me in place, choking on the scream as he buried those thick fingers inside me. My body lifted from the wall but he pushed me back and closed his mouth over my pussy, sucking and licking in all the right places, all at once.

Pleasure bloomed across every inch of me. I struggled to stand but he held me in place, working his fingers quickly as I panted into my hands. The scream in my throat built beyond anything I could control. Heat gushed between my legs as I snapped forward at the waist with the force of my orgasm. He surged upward, capturing my mouth with his and swallowed my scream.

The taste of my own pleasure slammed into my taste buds as his tongue invaded my mouth, lashing at the same rate his fingers plunged into me from below. Mason pinned me back into the alcove with his body, arched over me as I came for him a second time, drenching his hand, my pleasure lingering on his tongue and mine. I would have begged for more, anything, but I couldn't form more than a bare thought.

"Need you," I mumbled against his mouth.

"Damn, that's what I want to hear, gorgeous. But I'm gonna take you inside for that," he rasped against my mouth.

Our bodies broke contact for a second as he scooped to ground level and came back up with my key that worked for him like it hadn't for me minutes before, the traitorous thing. Mason's arm wrapped around me as he drew me into his chest, lifting me against his hard torso. His mouth never left mine as he slammed the door behind him, and flicked the lock.

"Where's your bedroom, Nyla?" His voice came out low and rough in the darkness, his oversized body bumping into walls he didn't know.

"Put me down," I murmured, running my hands along his chest. "Just for now," I added when he didn't budge.

"Mmhm," he muttered, releasing me with no small dose of reluctance.

"It's not a big place. Probably nothing like yours," I mused, finding his hand and leading him along the short hall and took the second left after Brady's room. "Here–"

I didn't get to take another breath before he was on me. Large hands cupped my jaw, tipping my head back. My lips parted—on a breath, or a word—that we shared for a fraction of a second before he covered my mouth in a deep kiss that left me leaning into him.

Mason still tasted of peat and whiskey, but with a hint of the chocolate dessert we shared before, and something sweeter now. His tongue swept across my lips, pushing deeper as his hands dropped to cradle me against him. He backed me up until my knees hit the bed and we folded together. All sense of gravity left me as we fell, but he never let me go. My skirt slipped aside as his knee pushed my thighs apart, one hand gripping my hip to haul us both further up the mattress. Fingers dug into my skin hard enough to bruise.

"Sorry, gorgeous. But fuck if I don't want you," he rasped, dragging his mouth from mine. Dark eyes pierced through me before he kissed me again, rough and untethered and wild.

This was the Mason Hale who terrified everyone else. The Mason Hale who was untouchable.

And here he was, in my bed, peeling clothes from my body even as he yanked his shirt over his head. I pushed up to trace my fingertips across his chest, memorizing every ridge of muscle as he worked my skirt over my legs with one hand. My thong never stood a chance. A flick of his wrist tore through the flimsy lace. I gasped at the ripping noise that echoed around my bedroom, jerking my gaze back to him.

"You don't need these around me, not on date night. Alright?" His mouth grazed over mine, his kiss searing.

"Alright," I whispered, back, breathless as I wriggled a few inches up the bed, desperate for space. Hell, I could barely breathe around this man.

Mason's hand clamped over my thigh, pinning me in place. "You're right where you need to be,

Nyla." Both hands ran up my body, along my arms to stretch them over my head. He pressed them into my pillow with one hand, tangling our fingers together. "Are you on birth control?"

"The shot." I pulled a hand free to rub at my arm subconsciously, but he growled and caught it again, pressing my hands back where they were before. "Mason?"

"I told you tonight was for you." His mouth covered mine, his kisses slow and long and deep as he nudged my thighs further apart. His belt jingled, and his jeans brushed my foot on their way to the floor.

Sensation flooded me as he drew his fingers across my slicked flesh, still damp from the mess we made there before. I mewled, lifting my hips when his touch disappeared, and he laughed.

"Good to know that's what you like," he murmured.

Heat flushed my cheeks. "I'm sorry, I have no idea what I'm doing," I mumbled, turning my head away as shame filled me.

The hand on my wrist flexed, paired with a sound that originated in his chest that seemed all consuming and utterly terrifying. "Don't hide from me, Nyla," he warned me. "Whatever that asshole did to you, that doesn't stand here. Not between us. Here, you're safe. Whoever you need to be, do you understand me?" The fingers that were coated in my pleasure caught my chin and turned my face gently to meet his unflinching gaze. Mason's tone softened. "I know he hurt you, gorgeous. Badly. But it doesn't have to be like that. I promise."

"You can't promise me things like that," I whispered, my heart thumping with something far too close to hope in my chest. "You *can't.*"

"I can." He kissed me again, spreading my legs wider. His tongue slid into my mouth as he pressed the head of his cock against my entrance and pushed.

My soaked, aching flesh gave, and he slid inside me. Every thrust sent shivers of tightly wound pleasure paired with sharp spikes of pain through me, though those lessened as Mason edged his way deeper into me, and my body let him in.

"Look at me," he demanded, arching over me. "Stay here with me, Nyla. We're right here. Nowhere else."

"Here," I whispered, folding my fingers around his, letting him pin my hands down, giving him control. My body softened as he pushed deeper, his hips meeting mine. A soft cry tore from me as I arched beneath him. I clenched around the thick intrusion, my legs tightening around his hips.

An approving noise emanated from deep in Mason's chest, and he began to move. Slow at first, then building up, our bodies arching together until the scream he suppressed before tore from me again.

This time he did nothing to stop those sounds as I shattered beneath him. My thighs wrapped around his waist, my heels digging into his ass. He caught my hip, running his thumb along the inside until I moaned at the sensitive touch.

"Fuck, you feel so good, fluttering around me," he groaned, tilting his head back, though his eyes were still on me. "Can you come for me again, gorgeous? Once more." He drove into me deeper, faster.

I swore I'd never not feel the shape of him branded inside me after tonight. I clawed at his hand, knowing I'd probably mark him, and decided I didn't care. Pleasure built inside me, over again as his hand closed around my breast, toying gently with the nipple. Fresh pleasure sliced through me, and it's all I needed. Heat gushed between my thighs, wetting me, him and the bed. I raised my head and cried out into his shoulder.

Mason slammed deep into me, my name a roar

on his lips as he shuddered above me, his breath coming in long pants. "Christ, girl. You're beyond beautiful." His hold wrapped around my hands gentled, his thumb stroking over my racing pulse points.

I didn't mind, lying beneath him wrapped in his arms with him still embedded inside me. Nearly every part of me ached, but in the best way. And there was no way in hell I would be moving before morning. Not for anything.

I sighed and nestled into him as he rolled us, reaching sideways.

"Nyla? Have you got some tissues or something? I don't want to ruin your bed."

I giggled and crawled over him to find the tissue box and propped the cold cardboard box onto his stomach. "Wish granted."

Okay, so I wouldn't be moving from now on for almost anything. Because this was perfect.

Mason leaned over me and pressed a kiss to my temple. "Definitely not moving. Though I can almost hear you thinking."

I batted him away and snuggled into his side, not bothering with the tissues, liking the feel of his brand inside me.

Yep, perfect.

CHAPTER ELEVEN

NYLA

I leaned over Mason's body as he lay back, his arms stretched behind his head, watching me. That was the deal we made an hour before. He hadn't let me touch him earlier, and now it was my turn.

Midnight eyes glittered as I knelt over him, taking the head of his swollen cock into my mouth and licked the tip. Breath hissed between his teeth, and the heavy length in my mouth thickened impossibly.

"Fuck, girl. You're gonna kill a man looking at me like that." His hands flexed on his elbows where they rested behind his head, but other than that, he made no movement at all.

"Good boy," I murmured, freeing my mouth up with an audible *pop*.

Mason groaned, and I watched his hands flex again, the corners of my mouth turning up. *Have a taste of your own medicine, Mister Hale.* I'd more than enjoyed what we did before, but I'd wanted to touch him, feel the warmth of him in my hands. This way, he got to understand that empty ache while I played as I wanted.

I leaned down, licking the length of him again, letting my fingertips tickle his balls.

"*Fuuuucckk,*" he groaned. His eyes flickered shut before he snapped them open to focus on me.

Another little rule we agreed on earlier.

Smiling, I opened my lips and swallowed his cock as deep as I could, swirling my tongue around the base of his length. He pulsed in my mouth even as he cursed fluently above me. Those rugby thighs I loved even more up close, muscle on muscle, tensed as I wiggled my way deeper into my spot, setting a rhythm that earned me enough moans until I struggled to breathe for the thickness of him.

Then I pulled my mouth off his length, licking my lips as I straddled him and leaned my hands over his arms.

"You're cruel, Nyla," Mason murmured, though

his flashing eyes told me he thought anything but that.

"Mmm, if you say so." I speared myself with his cock, sinking down onto him until he filled me and my thighs rested on his. "Oh, wow. You're so thick."

"And you're tight." He blew out air between his teeth in a quick blast. "Move for me, gorgeous, before I come just from the sensation of your wet pussy gripping my cock."

I levered myself up, using his arms for purchase, and dropped back down on him, working in a quick rhythm that set my insides ablaze with need. But even with the thickness of him inside me, I wouldn't be able to come without something a little more at this angle. "Mason—" I whispered as I dropped a hand between us, rubbing my clit.

"That's it. Show me what you like." He held himself perfectly still for me. "Show me how that wet pussy of yours creams for me, Nyla."

I bit my lip, my body overheating under his study. His gaze ate up everything I did so hungrily. I wasn't used to anyone watching me, or even caring that I took pleasure for myself during sex. But that he did, and from the feeling of how hard he was inside me, got off on it...

I folded forward, crying out as I came. He caught me, wrapping me in a tight embrace.

"That's it. Come around my cock, gorgeous. Fuck, you feel so good." Mason held onto me tighter, pushing up gently from below.

I gasped at the sensation that rocketed through me, then vaguely remembered our pact. "The rules! You said you wouldn't—"

"Touch you until you took your own pleasure. And that looked like plenty right there. Are you gonna let me make you come hard again now?" He pulled me deep onto him, pushing up until I was impaled on his length and held me there, imprisoned with his hands on my hips. "Nyla?"

I gasped, wiggling my hips, but I could barely speak. Waves of pleasure rippled through me as I struggled to breathe, struggled to move. Every time I shifted, another shot of pure bliss hit me.

Mason's slow smile was beyond devastating. "Come for me, gorgeous. Just like this. Ride me again, and then I'm going to fuck you deep and fast."

I nodded, rolling my hips with his encouragement, though he didn't move at all. I groaned as he pushed me down deeper onto him. My nails scraped at his shoulders. I rode him like he demanded, grinding onto him as I panted until the waves broken and I—

Shattered.

I clung to him, almost sobbing with the over-whelm as he kissed me gently. Our lips moved sweetly, tongues tangling in a slow dance.

"That was beautiful. Do you remember my promise?"

I blinked up at him, my heart starting to slow as I leaned against him in a pool of sweat, every limb languid. "No?"

He laughed and tucked me against him, folding my hands behind his neck. "Hold on to me, okay?"

"Okay—" That one single word became a scream I couldn't control as he slammed into me from below, over and over and over. I guessed I was about to find out how sound proofed—or not—my walls were because the man beneath me was beyond relentless. I clung to him, my nails digging into his skin as he railed me, fucking me hard and fast without ever shifting his position from where he sat beneath me.

I buried my face in his neck, breathing him in as I panted and muffled my cries against his skin, but he wound his hand in my hair, and pulled.

"I want to hear you scream for me, Nyla. Know

you're mine tonight," he grated, never stopping, his fingers digging into my hip like he branded me with his touch.

And so I screamed for him, coming again like I couldn't stop. My thighs clamped around his hips, locking me in place. I thought I'd never stop shivering, my entire body trembling by the time he slammed hilt deep and roared my name above me.

The hand tangled in my hair clasped my head to his chest. His heart pounded rapidly against my cheek as I lapped salt from his skin. Mason collapsed backward bringing me with him.

"Damn girl. I think I'm in love with you."

"Mmmmm." I made a long, contented sound, because nothing else wanted to come out right then.

He laughed, holding me to him as something vibrated on the floor. "Ah, they can go to hell. Probably Hansen telling me to get on with it."

"Mmm. Or reminding me to move my car." I yawned and snuggled into his chest.

How good could a man possibly feel? I'd never had the luxury of sleeping with a man before in my life. Stuart refused flat out, sleeping on his side of the bed and never touched me after our brief rounds of one-sided sex that left me more than wanting. He proposed to me straight out of high school and we divorced shortly after having Brady because family life wasn't what his mother sold to him. Funny, that. A pity that his toxic traits drove mine away...not that this moment was the time to reflect on my shitty past.

I yawned again, sinking into Mason's embrace. The vibrating stopped and started again a moment later.

"Fuck. Off," Mason enunciated clearly for a man who should be exhausted. I frowned and shifted in his arms, straining for the edge of the bed. "Ignore them, gorgeous. The boys get rowdy on a Saturday night. Prank calls are the name of the game." He stroked my hair back from my face in a tender motion I wanted to savour forever.

But that vibration twigged something low in my stomach. "Not if it's not yours ringing." I elbowed him not so lightly in the stomach. He grunted and let me go. The cool spots where he had held me a moment before sank in as I scampered over him, naked, to get to my phone. I reached my purse and fumbled a hand inside in the darkness just as it stopped vibrating.

Finally I found the device and stared at the number that I missed twice, my stomach sinking. *Lisa.* Times two at one a.m. plus change. Brady's babysitter who my sister-in-law insisted we still use so she could go to bed whenever she wanted for the night.

My thumb hit the *call* button without thinking. "Lisa?" I thumbed the speaker button and went searching for my panties then realised they got destroyed earlier and hunted for a fresh pair.

"He's not here, Nyla. I'm so sorry. I don't know what to do. I looked everywhere!" Lisa's hysterical sobbing left me colder than the wet spot I tried to avoid on the other side of the mattress earlier.

I grabbed for my clothes, shoving them on in the darkness. Something tore. I threw the black skirt aside, reaching for my trusty jeans. "It's okay, Lisa," I lied. "I'm sure he's somewhere about." *At two in the morning?* "Is Claire there?"

"I'm here." My sister in law's cold voice closed over the hysterical babysitter's. *Good to know someone keeps their head in an emergency.* "What the hell sort of bullshit did you bring to my house? You're lucky he's my brother's child," she snarled.

I closed my eyes. *Or not. Family sucks.* Mason's arm wrapped around my chest from behind, pulling me into a tight embrace. I squeezed his shoulder and gently disentangled myself, but kept a hold of his hand, grateful for his support as my panic skyrocketed. He frowned at me, flicking a bedside table lamp on.

He's looking for you? Mason wrote on the screen of his phone, showing me the illuminated display.

I shrugged. That had been my thought too, but I didn't think he'd climb out of bed in the middle of the night for that. Brady knew I was out with Mason, and he loved his coach, supported my relationship with him. At least, I thought he did.

"Did you hear him leave?" I asked the phone to a general silence, willing myself to remain calm despite my own raging panic as I shoved my legs into my oldest jeans and gratefully grabbed the t-shirt that Mason tossed my way.

The only response for the first few seconds was Lisa's muted sobs and Claire's hushed snarls. Mason's arm wrapped tight around me as he battled his own clothes one handed. He tipped my head back and kissed me hard, still not speaking but the message passed between us with clarity as he tucked me tight into his side and finished dressing.

We'll find him. You're not alone.

Never in my life had I been so relieved to have someone on my team. Someone like Mason.

"No," came Claire's clipped answer.

Short and sweet, and utterly useless.

I swallowed a dollop of pure fear. "Thank you. Have you called the police?"

"What for?"

I closed my eyes and blew out a breath. "Because a child in your care has gone missing, Claire. He's either walked away, or—" My eyes flew open and met Mason's narrowed gaze head on.

"Or someone took him." Mason finished the sentence for me.

"Who is that? Who are you talking to?" Claire snapped.

We both ignored her.

Mason's mouth set in a hard line, the lights from the city outside leaving his face in harsh relief. He placed the keys to his truck in my hand. "Where would he take Brady, Nyla?"

Stuart.

Clarity slapped me with a side dish of revenge that only an ex could manage.

Oh, my God. This is payback for me walking out on him last week. He's taken my son.

Our son, who can't stand to be in the same room as his father because he was scared of him.

I should have listened better.

I shook my head. "I– I have no idea. I don't know anything about his life anymore." I looked at him helplessly. "I tried my best to stay away." Because I thought it best to keep my distance. And now that choice was biting my ass in spectacular fashion.

"Who are you talking about?" Claire demanded.

I sighed. "I'm sorry we bothered you, Claire," I said softly. "Go back to sleep. I'll call the police and handle it."

"As you should." Her voice remained cold, and I expected the line to go dead.

Instead, Lisa's sobs grew louder. "Stuart took him, didn't he?" she whispered, her voice ragged.

I froze. "What do you know, Lisa?" My heart pounded in my chest as Mason shoved mismatched socks on my feet, one feeling thicker than the other, and stuffed them into old shoes I hadn't worn in years, but I didn't care. "What happened?"

"He– he called me. Yesterday. Told me to make sure I was with Brady last night. I didn't want to take your money, Nyla. I knew you didn't have a job right now," she wailed.

My blood solidified in my veins. "Lisa," I said carefully, plating my ass on my bed as gravity took a dive, and took me with it. "Can you please tell me where you think Brady and St– his dad are right now?"

Anything. Give me any information you have. Please. Tell me he's safe.

"The restaurant. He's— He was so angry with you," she hiccupped. "I'm so sorry."

The call went dead in my hand. One moment I was holding a phone and keys, the next I sat in Mason's truck, and he was strapping me into the passenger seat, talking on his phone in a low, urgent voice.

"Yeah, that themed restaurant we were at for the team Christmas dinner. Anyone you can. Police, whoever you can get. Thanks, man. I owe you what, ten now?" he laughed and there was no humour in it as I stared at him.

"Mason?"

He leaned in and kissed me as he hung up. "We're gonna get him back, gorgeous. I promise."

I nodded as he headed around the front of the truck. The engine roared to life in the silent suburb. Streets and lights melded into a blur as we headed across the city, toward the restaurant I thought I had left for the last time. I knew long before we got there how this would end, because that was the thing about promises.

You should never make a vow you couldn't keep.

CHAPTER TWELVE

MASON

The back of the restaurant was quiet. No cars sat in the lot, and the door was unlocked. Two things that roiled my blood on different levels. I kept Nyla behind me where she pressed to my back. Her fingernails dug into my skin, not that I cared or felt the pain. I figured the asshole would either be in the office she'd told me was upstairs, one of the few pieces of information I got out of her on the way across town before she shut down on me completely, or he'd be in the bar, drinking himself into a stupor, or worse.

That this was where Stuart chose to bring Brady terrified me. It had all the makings of a really shitty situation that could turn on us at any point. I wrapped my hand around Nyla's, checking each darkened booth decorated with western and cowboy paraphernalia as we walked quietly through the restaurant, but long before we reached the bar, I knew it was empty.

The smallest sound from the mezzanine where we'd hosted the team Christmas party drew my attention back to the stairs and the level above. A second sound froze me, a shift in the flooring over our heads. It could have been the older building settling, or—

"Stuart, get off me! Help"

My heart shattered fresh on the spot.

"I told you to call me Dad!" Something glass broke on the floor above us, the sound shattering the silence at our level.

I barely moved before Nyla sprinted forward. Her black hair whipped past me as I cursed myself for putting sandshoes on her feet for the briefest second. Then I was after her, my feet pounding the boards, all thought of remaining stealthy out the window. I hit the stairs when she was already at the top and powered after her, only to collide with her back a moment later.

"Stuart, you can't have Brady tonight. It's not your night," she said in a completely reasonable voice, walking in a wide circle around the man rather than directly at him, like I hadn't just run into her and nearly knocked her clean over. "Brady, why don't you come over here?"

Brady, bless him, crouched low and did exactly what his mother asked, scampering around Stuart's uncoordinated swing. The kid skidded on glistening liquid that spread across the floor amidst sharp glass shards—the carnage we'd heard below that looked like the remnants of a spirits bottle. The boy crashed into his mother who hugged him, swiped her hands across his face, and sent him straight back to me without looking.

Now that's trust.

I prayed I could keep safe what she'd just gifted to me.

"You okay, bud?" I knelt, holding out my arms.

Brady nodded and slammed into my shoulder with all the energy of an overstimulated, hyperactive kid awake after midnight for all the wrong reasons. I folded my arms around his lean frame. My heart clenched down hard as I watched Nyla approach Stuart. The other man stumbled about in a circle and tripped over his own feet to land heavily on the floor. I knew there was nothing I could do to help her right now. This was her battle, as long as she wanted to fight it. All I could do was support her and protect the most precious thing in her world.

She crouched in front of Stuart, her hair pooling on the floor around them both, speaking softly as blue and red lights lit up the glassed front of the restaurant. I leaned back against the wall near the stairwell, the echoes of the night I flirted hard with the woman opposite me back when she was dressed in a reindeer costume overlaid with the vision of her now in plain jeans and a black long sleeved tee I'd pulled out of some drawer and thrown over her head in a moment of need.

Brady clung to me as I settled on the floor to wait.

"Are they going to take my dad away?" he asked without a single stutter.

I looked straight in his face and promised silently that I'd never lie to him. "Yeah, mate. They will. I have no idea what happened after that, but we can figure that out together, however long your mum says it's okay for me to stick around, alright?"

"She better say you can be around forever." Brady settled beside me and held out his hand. "You got a phone? I know a great game to download."

I snorted and fished out my phone from my jeans. "Sure. But if you get me into trouble, you're up for stair runs with me when Coach tells me I've done the wrong thing. Deal?"

"You mean I can train with you?" Brady's eyes glowed.

Okay, so not my finest moment. I cleared my throat as bootsteps thundered up the stairs I prayed would hold up for one more night. The closer I looked at the restaurant that Nyla used to work in, the more holes and issues I saw in it, and the happier I was that she'd have nothing to do with the place after tonight.

I braced a hand above Brady's head to protect him from the oncoming cops in case they didn't spot him, glancing over to let the first person up the stairs know we were there, and then down at the kid attempting to hack into my phone for all he was worth.

"Alright, bud. What's this game and how much trouble am I gonna be in with your mum?"

His brilliant smile told me all the things I didn't want to know as Leon, Hansen and my teammates surrounded us, forming an honour guard that stood between us and the rest of the world.

I just had to wait until Nyla was done so our protective bubble could include her too.

A week after Stuart was removed from Nyla's, she was offered a job at Hansen's restaurant as he suddenly desired an extra chef and a new front of house manager. Both Nyla and Chaz accepted the work, and they integrated into Hansen's team seamlessly.

Brady spent the week getting me into trouble on various fronts and found it hilarious when Nyla caught 'us' out doing the wrong thing. We'd had a few chats but I still seemed to be a big brother figure to him more than anything else. I could live with that, provided I didn't piss Nyla off too much. Because today was kinda big.

Big, in the way of the charity match where I currently had another local team running directly at me. We were three points down in the fourth quarter with less than two minutes left on the clock. The other team were happy to dilly-dally their way along the field and waste time to run their time out, but I was keen to end this game on a high note. We didn't even need a converted try to put this sucker to bed. Just a ball over the line would do it.

I watched the ball play, but a flicker of red and black—my colours—caught my attention in my peripherals. Brady waved a giant hand drawn pennant of a Ninja stabbing a sloth that I suspected was meant to depict the Sanford Sentinels beating the other team. Nyla held her hands up in a *what can you do* movement. I huffed a laugh, and caught the yell aimed at me along with movement coming my way in time to turn my attention back to the game and not earn myself a falcon in the face.

I didn't fumble the ball, and I didn't get my ass ploughed by the opposition, but I did manage to take a clean intercept right through a gap between two players who watched me pass between them like they were standing still.

Because I sure as hell wasn't.

The moment that ball was in my arms, my body worked on automatic exactly as it had been trained to do. I sprinted the length of the field close to the sideline, aware of someone running alongside me matching me pace for pace, but I didn't look back because I didn't need to. That tryline was there, and then I was over it, the ball planted firmly in the mucky, muddy grass that had already taken a pounding, my hand wrapped securely around the ball.

My brain registered the ref's whistle and the

horn for the end of the game, and more than one body crashed into mine.

But all I saw was Brady bouncing up and down, cheering for all he was worth. Nyla stood beside him, a brilliant smile spread over her stunning face as she cheered right alongside him.

And that was all I wanted to see in the world.

EPILOGUE

MASON

For all the post game celebrations, the politics and talks afterwards, gifting to the charity, and close off for the unofficial season, it didn't take long for the grounds to clear out. I waited until last with Leon, making sure I had showered and sprayed myself with enough deodorant to kill a locker room.

I bounced on my toes, still full of nervous energy despite my deadened thighs from that last run that no scalding shower or rub down would help. I'd stretched plenty, listened to Coach's secondary pep talk that was for me alone, but for this next part no one could help me with, but me.

Any maybe one other, but that part would come a little later on.

"If you keep jumping around, you're gonna need another shower," Leon stared at me, looking more like a father figure than my trainer. Or maybe they were the same thing. I had a few of those, but he came on board as an extra a few years back and just sort of stayed.

Even Hansen had a few words of his own for me before he left. That talk had been nerve wracking enough.

"Alright. You think everyone's gone?" I peered around the outside of the door, but the stands were deserted as far as I could see.

"You'd better get moving or she'll be gone, too." Leon clapped my shoulder hard enough to rock me forward onto my toes.

I took the hint and stepped out of the tunnel for the last time that night. The sun had started setting, leaving a slim strip of light above the horizon, through a deep haze had settled over the grounds. I closed my eyes and swallowed hard. If I screwed this up, I knew Nyla wouldn't give me a second chance. I glanced back at Leon who gave me an encouraging nod.

"It's okay to risk it all when everything is worth the risk," he murmured.

I grinned. "You should get that tattooed over

your heart, Coach."

"Who said I don't already have it somewhere else?" He sauntered away, flicking the giant floods on as he left me alone.

The grounds illuminated, but that would leave outside the stadium still dim enough that...

Ah, hell. I just needed to balls up and do this.

I pushed one hand into my pocket to reassure myself and jogged around the outside of the stadium to the parking lot. The whole place was deserted and after the brightness of the floodlights, it took me a moment to see the single car left in the lot.

I slowed to a walk, heading over to Brady and Nyla. Brady stuffed a hotdog into his face while Nyla leaned against her car.

"Are you always the last one out?"

I shrugged. "I thought you gave me that spiel once. Wasn't it 'first one in, last to leave' or something like that?"

"Yeah. Something like that." She tipped her head to one side as I leaned down to kiss her. "I have a night off, and Brady seems to be wide awake...if you're not dead on your feet."

"Yeah. I know you have the night off." A lump grew in my throat I couldn't get around.

Nyla studied my face. "Are you okay?"

"That was a great try, Mason! You really ripped up the grass." Brady mimed skidding across the car park on his tummy.

"Ah, that." I winced. The groundskeepers would be fixing my dive divot for the next week or two. "Don't lose your hotdog, okay? I just want to talk to your mum for a moment. You remember that game on my phone?" I passed the device over.

"Oh yeah! The one with the monster trucks, and..." Brady was off and running with his current obsession.

"Yeah, that one." I coughed into my fist.

Nyla was still watching me. "What are you doing?"

"What?" I tried to look innocent and completely fucked it up. "I know I haven't known you for too long, but—"

"Mason." Nyla folded her arms. "There are better places to break up with me."

"What?" I squinted at her. "Sh– No. *No*. That's not what I'm— Dammit." I dropped to one knee and managed to extract the ring box from my pocket at the same time without fumbling the velvet. "This is the opposite. I'm just better with actions than I am with words." I took a deep breath when she said nothing, though her eyes widened. Actually, I couldn't remember the last time I left her speechless outside the bedroom, and I wasn't sure if that boded good or bad right now, so I just ploughed right ahead. "It's been a few weeks, no, a month since we met." *Okay, words aren't my only weakness. Let's add math in there too.* "It's been a massive whirlwind. I fell in love with you fast, Nyla. And I'm not letting go anytime soon, not unless you tell me you don't want me around. I love you, and I love Brady. You're both the two most important people in my world. Honestly, I can't imagine my world without you in it. This afternoon, I nearly screwed up a game because we were talking in the middle of it. And after that try, you two were the first faces I looked for. You say you don't have a family but...I think you come preloaded with one. If you want it. So..." I managed to inhale part of a breath and flicked the ring box open to display the solitaire emerald cut diamond set in a bezel that she'd be able to wear for work, or so the jeweller assured me when he designed it. "I'd love it if you would marry me. And let me maybe try out being Brady's stand-in dad, if you'd let me, and if that's okay with him."

Please.

Nyla stared at me with her mouth open while my knees ached and my thighs throbbed. Somewhere in the back, Leon threw the floods on for the parking lot and blinded me. I still didn't move.

Please say something. Please react. Please, please, please.

Please.

"I think it's a good idea," Brady piped up from the back of the car, his mouth full of hotdog.

"Shhh," Nyla hushed him and turned back to me. "I— I thought." Nothing else came out, and her mouth closed.

"I know," I managed, wondering if I would ever be able to stand upright at this rate or if I'd have to roll out of the crouch. "You've got all of my heart, Nyla. I promise. And all of my family, too. Every part." Both my team and my actual family had adopted Nyla straight in, which was typical of both of all the people I loved, probably because they gave love the same way I did.

Openly and unconditional.

I wondered belatedly if that scared the shit out of her and if I should have maybe prepared a different sort of speech.

"Yes," she whispered.

I blinked. "Can you say that again please?"

She caught my wrists and hauled me upright. Several things popped and I hoped nothing hurt because I was a bit numb all over. Nyla grabbed my shirt and pulled me down for a long kiss. "I said yes, Mason," she whispered.

"Oh, good." I gathered her into my arms, crushing her into my chest and inhaled the cloud of frangipani and other sweet things that seemed to float around her in a giant cloud. Turning her in my arms, I managed to wiggle the ring onto her finger the way Hansen coached me, and then kissed the tips—my own touch, not his. "Because I really do love you and didn't want you to say no."

She snuggled into my shoulder, her tears dripping onto the back of my hand. "I thought—"

"I know. I'm terrible at this stuff."

She shook her head. "No, you're not. I'm just really ruined."

I shrugged. "So, we have some healing to do. All of us. And we do it together, okay?"

"Okay," she whispered back. "I—" Nyla took a deep breath, and her words ran together. "*Iloveyoutoo.*"

"I know, gorgeous."

My girl might be a bit broken, but I hadn't lied to her either. That really was okay and I was here for her every step of the way, whatever that looked like. I kissed her again until something nudged my thigh.

I looked down to find one of the training balls I'd been missing for the last week proffered out the window of her car by sticky hotdog sauce fingers.

"Uh, Mason? Since you're gonna be my new dad, can you sign my ball, please?"

AT THE OTHER END

A second Author's Note

Thanks so much for reading Mason and Nyla's story in ARROGANT RUCKING PLAYER. Their story is full of heartstrings that pulled all the way out. There's a few things I wanted to mention before you go based around my love of sport and Mason's history.

I grew up watching sport with my grandma (Nanna) that covered quite a few bases, but rugby was one of her faves. She didn't however, have a favourite team picked (this was back in the days of pulling the TV guide out of the newspaper and high-lighting her choices of the week—her ability alone, she was the TV goddess of the house!). How the team we supported that night went by which team she thought was the 'cleanest' looking when they all ran out of the tunnel at the beginning of the game.

Now let's remember this was in the Eighties. Big hair was the trend for both men and women, and HAIR. HAPPENED. Also, tighty-whities. Nanna wasn't a fan of ink, so tattoos were out, but oh boy, could she crush on muscle men of all sorts.

A note on language—there's a lot of Aussie in this book. Yes, sparrowfart is real, and it happens just before dawn. Our currency and coins look different, blue rinses still do happen though they aren't as popular as they once were, and dilly dallying takes all day long.

Mason's history spawns from a slightly different experience. In the early 2000s I went on my first cruise that also happened to be the first cruise ship to visit a particular tiny Fijian island (there are three hundred and thirty-two). This island is only five kilometres long by two kilometres wide. At the time, we took a tiny tender (small motorboat with a flat bottom to traverse shallow water) off the larger ship that moored further out in deeper water and motored up to the beach. There was very little on the island apart from a few homes and a church, a post office, a gorgeous green pool and on the other side, a lovely crescent beach. We were met at the time by a handful of lovely young men who were tasked with showing the visitors around their island. Everyone else was in church. The island had one TV in the post office. The young man who was our guide was an amazing person who loved his island. He was very passionate and wanted to play soccer for Fiji. He was the inspiration for Mason when I planned this story out, and the character developed from that single seed. This boy, who was about seventeen at the time, took the truly crappily drawn mud map the ship had provided (a marker, photocopied hand drawn A4 (letter size) sheet) and nearly leapt out of his skin.

> "This is my island?" he asked,
>   pointing to the paper, his face
>   alight.
> I smiled, nodding and tapped the
>   point marked green pool. "Yes, can
>   you show us this?"
> But he was stuck on the bigger
>   picture. "But this is my island?"
> And it hit me—he was seeing a
>   picture of his island for the first
>   time.

Perspective is a wonderful gift. The young man showed us so many parts of his island that honestly we probably weren't supposed to see—walking us down muddy paths behind houses, showing us his neighbours' pigs and piglets (we get a glimpse into Mason's early life during his date with Nyla, but I wanted to tell this story here), all the way to the beach on the other side of the island. We learned so much. It was amazing. He talked about the girl he liked and would ask to the next island dance (she had *curves* and that was a critical point!) and he loved playing soccer. The thought of leaving his island made him both sad and happy at the same time.

That memory has stayed with me for the last few decades and I remember it more strongly than the rest of the trip together. The ship paid for our visit in giant oversized bags of rice and potatoes that couldn't be grown on the island. The women, after church, plucked at my handbag and Mum's bracelet (each made of cork and wood, which we both ended up giving and emptying out) because they wanted to figure out how to pull the crafted parts apart to make to sell as that was how they made money and sold to tourists and other islands at the time.

Today, that island has a full contingent of resorts,

a large jetty and I couldn't find the green pool in photos. And that makes me...sad. Because the island that I saw, the one that was this boy's home, and now Mason—it doesn't exist anymore. All names have been retracted and changed.

Thank you again for reading Mason's story. I wanted to share the history of where his inspiration originated with you because stories should be shared, although I feel the island boy's story should be told in voices, not just on the page. Sharing stories is an old tradition. The only other person who experienced that with me was Mum, and her memories have gone now too. I'd hate to see his story be lost to time because I didn't share it with you too.

Sofia xx

ABOUT THE AUTHOR

USA Today Bestselling author Sofia Aves writes fast-paced police romances, sizzling military units, steamy cowboys with a Montana backdrop and the occasional cheeky god. Sofia writes kidlit for charity and has over one hundred and fifty publications across five not-so-super-secret pen names. As acquisitions editor for Evernight and Evernight Teen publishing she loves discovering new talent in romance and YA spaces, and is a mum of three crazies in a returned veteran household. Sofia has two overly large fur babies who think they're teacup puppies, a duck who prefers to eat from a dog bowl and two axolotls named after a dragon and a firebird.

Sofia lives near Brisbane, Australia where she has her own alpaca park, Lorendel.

www.sofiaaves.com

Sign up to Sofia's newsletter and get a free Blue Blooded Brothers book.

Haven't read the Z Boy's prequel? Get it for free here:
A TABLE FOR TEN

Follow Sofia on
BookBub
Twitter
Instagram

READ SOFIA'S SERIES

Blue Blooded Brothers
Collision

Politics & Paperwork

Blindsided

Sentinel

Mugshots & Candy Canes

Impact

Reckoning

Red Hart Ranch

Snow on the Range

Siren on the Range

Sundown on the Range

Spirit on the Range

Ash on the Range (2025)

Mistletoe on the Range (2025)

Forgotten Mountain Man

Texan Devils

Ranger's Wish

Ranger Bedevilled

Ranger's Passion

Ranger's Fury

Ranger's Wrath

Ranger's Storm

Snapdragons & Seductions

Summer with a Ranger

Merry with a Ranger

Playing to Win

Off Boarding

Vicious Slash

Zero Pointer

Off Stage Fling

Rippton Allstars

Crushing It

Glacial Force

· · ·

Rippton Creatives
Study Games
Make Me, Break Me
Twisted Obsession
Spring Break with a Mafia Prince
A Royally Fake French Menage

Jericho Chimeras
Puck Me Always
Puck My Heart
Puck me Sideways

Z Boys
King
Joker
Hearts
Ace
Mayhem & Mistletoe
Ruski

Fast Track to Love

Speed Trap

Klauss Brothers
Zander
Keegan

Gallo Empire *with Jade Marshall*
Splintered Vows
Fractured Vows
Fierce Vows
Savage Covenant

Rom Coms
She's A Hot Christmas Mess
Boats, Moats and Root Beer Floats

Writing Romantasy as
SOFIA SHELLEY
Dead Poets Sorority

Writing Reverse Harem Dark Romance as

DOVE PRIEST

Recurve Ridge

Kidlit writing as

JO SEYSENER

The OCD Elf

Greg and the Egg

writing YA as

JOSS PHOENIX

Alchem Academy (2025)

Writing spicy paranormal romance as

RAVEN HUSH

Club Fray

Darkest Desires

Purge

Kidnapped By Claws

Ruin

.   .   .

Shadow Lords

Sinner's End

Heaven's Gate (2026)

Monster Brides

Phoenix's Eternal Flame

Kraken's Vow

Krampus' Christmas Bride

Silent Sentinels Duet

Reflections of Silence

Echoes in the Void

Monsters In New York

Feral Moon Rising (2025)